D1743129

FranKie B
all Hallows Keep

ANDiE LOW

Squabbling Sparrows Press

ISBN: 978-0-9951235-4-0

1

Frankie settles back into the softly upholstered sofa that dominates the cabin on the tugboat *Annie,* home to Stanley Morris, leader of the Marina Coven. She can't believe she's this close to finding her missing dad when yet another obstacle has been thrown in her way. Not that Mimi Merriweather, time-lord, will be a challenge, surely. The woman must be ancient and Frankie's unable to get past an image of a gray-haired little old lady wearing sensible shoes.

Frankie leans forward, looking at Stanley who's sitting opposite her. "She can't be that much of a handful, can she?"

"She's that, and more." Stanley crosses his arms tightly over his chest and Frankie can't decide if he's signalling an end to their conversation, or it's a subconscious means of protection.

Her gaze swings to Zane, who chooses that moment to plonk himself in the chair next to Stanley. Frankie has grown used to Zane being around after all the weeks of sparring and magic practice together, yet she still knows very little about him other than that he's part merman and disturbingly good looking. She raises an eyebrow just like he does to her and waits. She isn't sure why she thinks Zane and Mimi have a history, but as always when her gut tingles, she listens.

Zane jumps to his feet again. "Yeah, I've just realized I left the printouts of Calico Jack's amulet back at my place." Before Frankie has a chance to quiz him further, he disappears.

To be honest, on hearing about the new roadblock in the quest to find her dad, Frankie had forgotten about the printouts of her grandad's amulet too. Not that this is all Zane will have to print out.

Frankie's attention settles back on the coven leader. "What is it you're not telling me?" Even if she wasn't in possession of magical powers, Frankie would know she's not getting the full story.

"Well, it's like this." Stanley goes quiet as though searching for the right words. Or maybe any words. "Mimi and I were for a time." Stanley shifts uncomfortably in his seat before quietly adding, "Married."

Frankie doesn't know whether to stand up or slump back, eventually opting for the latter. Of all the things she's been expecting Stanley to say, this isn't one of them. "Married? Does this mean?" Frankie twists around so she can see the terrarium that's currently prison to the lizard formerly known as Gwen, Stanley's daughter. Frankie still thinks life as a lizard is too good for the evil witch with the woman having killed three witches and tried for Frankie herself.

"I'm afraid so. Gwen had just turned two when Mimi decided being the wife of the coven leader didn't give her access to enough power. She left in search of a stronger mate, taking my daughter with her."

And just like that the pieces start to fall into place. Mimi having connections to both the coven and the Garnet family provides the link that's been missing. Seems odd though that Stanley's ex would latch onto the Garnet patriarch whose main strength is money. To be sure he's got lots of it, but the power of wealth pales compared to the power of magic. At least in Frankie's mind.

Only after Stanley has been speaking non-stop

for five minutes like she's his therapist, does Frankie realize Zane hasn't returned. He's either having major printer troubles, or he's avoiding her and any unpleasant questions. Even though she knows Zane's a lot older than he looks, for him to have been mixed up with Stanley's ex-wife is bizarre at best. Even Stanley looks to be avoiding the subject, having picked up the small chest Frankie found at *Garnet Cove* — make that Bonny Island — examining it forensically.

She's mulling over what else she can ask about Mimi Merriweather and by extension Gwen, when Zane reappears. That he's empty-handed points to there being a problem with the files Frankie sent to his printer.

Zane paces up and down in the small space available to him. "They've gone. It's gone. I don't understand it. My place should be as secure as any bank vault."

Frankie eventually sticks her foot out to stop him in his tracks. "Would you relax? If the files got lost in transit, I copied the email to myself when I sent them to your printer. It'll be a piece of cake to send them again."

"Yeah, well I'll need to get another printer for that to happen. Whoever it was didn't just take the files they took the whole blasted printer."

Stanley puts the small chest back down on the coffee table and turns to Zane. "With the wards you've got on your place, that shouldn't be possible."

"That's what I thought too." Zane smacks his first into the palm of his other hand, his frustration at having been burglarized evident.

Zane concentrating on something Frankie isn't privy to, she has to wave in order to get his attention. "But surely, whoever it was managing to break into your place narrows it down to someone who's got magical powers rather than some random having ripped you off."

Now Stanley is looking as agitated as Zane himself. "You know what you're saying don't you, Frankie?"

Frankie shrugs. "That it was an inside job?

The old man leans forward and retrieves *The Lore of Crafte* from the shelf under the coffee table, placing the coven's law book face down on its gleaming mahogany surface. He opens the back cover, plus a couple more pages, revealing a list of coven members.

It's a surprise for Frankie to see how long the list is, with it running to three full pages. Certainly there are more names listed than vessels tied up at Pier 51. The one thing every entry has in common is the beautiful copperplate lettering, even for Frankie's recently added name. That the writing is the same for every entry, tells of Stanley being in charge for a very long time.

Without a clue as to who most of these people are, Frankie fidgets impatiently, knowing it's down to Zane and Stanley to go through the list. They start with the first name, eliminating anyone who isn't strong enough to break the powerful wards Zane has on every entrance to his houseboat. On seeing stars next to more than a few names, Frankie can keep quiet no longer. She taps one of the stars. "What do these mean?"

"They are..." Stanley struggles to find the right words.

Rather than wait for the coven leader to find them, Zane butts in. "They're no longer... with us."

Frankie opens her mouth to push for more information. On seeing Stanley's haunted expression, she clamps her mouth shut, not wanting to add to the old guy's obvious pain. This isn't to say she won't pump Zane for more information later.

They move quickly after this, until there are three names left. Zane, Stanley, and Calico Jack.

Frankie isn't surprised. Her missing zombie warlock of a grandfather is the one most likely to benefit from getting his hands on the files she sent to Zane's printer. "Ha. Once a pirate, always a blimmin' pirate."

No doubt the crafty old barnacle had this in mind when he allowed Frankie to take photographs of the front and back of his amulet in the first place. This must have been the subject of the silent conversation he had with Anne, Frankie's grandmamma. Before this he'd been hedging on letting Frankie take any photos.

Imagine his surprise on checking the files to see her six photographs of the map. Especially with the 3D overlay he'd created above the table at the *Garnet Cove* jungle villa. If it wasn't for Frankie knowing about the copies stored safely somewhere in the cloud, she'd be well ticked off. Never mind if she's a little vague as to exactly which cloud and how to retrieve them. It's not like her nefarious relative even needs the photos, with him having scarpered with the original map.

"The one plus I can see in any of this is that Calico Jack and Anne Bonny don't know we've still got copies of everything." Frankie's smile after saying this is borderline evil – at least she hopes so as this is how she's feeling toward her only living-ish relatives.

The files missing, Frankie decides against mentioning the photos of the map. There's no point saying anything until she's seen printouts herself. She'd been in such a hurry to take the photos they could be blurry for all she knows. Her having deleted them from her phone immediately after, means she hasn't been able to check them either.

She also likes the idea of looking at them on her own in the peace and quiet. This way she's more likely to see things than if she's in a noisy environment like *Magic Beans* café or on the *Annie* with Zane and Stanley.

They're no further ahead when their meeting finishes. Frankie and Zane depart soon after, leaving Stanley to feed live cockroaches to his inmates. Frankie finds a perverse pleasure in thoughts of Gwen having to crunch her way through these. The nasty witch's other option would be to go hungry and put up with the scuttling bugs as room-mates. It serves the evil harridan right for trying to seize control of the coven from her dad.

Not that Gwen is alone in the terrarium. The other lizard inmate is none other than George Garnet, the man responsible for the death of Frankie's mom. The reason he's still among the living is because he's got answers, answers to questions that could well lead Frankie to Mimi Merri-weather, or even her father.

Frankie says goodbye to Zane at his front door, crosses the pier and walks onto the dock next to *The Crate*. This is the name she'd given to the rusty shipping container sitting off-center on an even rustier barge when it was her home. This was before she moved onto the *American Pearl*, the ghost ship she'd commandeered from the twice-dead Captain Garnet. Her knock is answered promptly by *The Crate's* newest tenant, Magda, the energy vamp. Dex is nowhere in sight.

"He's comatose again, isn't he?" It's the same whenever Dex spends time with Magda. It's not that the Jack Russell has the energy sucked out of him, rather he overdoses on the muffins Magda is so keen on feeding to him. For a meat eater, Dex has a very sweet tooth.

"Come on Dex, you know what'll happen if you put on too much weight."

"Awww, mom. The tastiest thing about those diet biscuits is the box they come in."

Despite him whining like a two-year-old, Dex stumbles to his feet and is soon following her down the pier in the direction of the *American Pearl*. As always, on seeing the sleek, two-masted schooner they both call home, Frankie's heart beats a little faster. She's never been a home-owner before and doubts the pleasure is going to wear off any time soon. On climbing aboard she's pleased to sense that she and Dex are the only living beings on board. Apart that is, from a few spiders and one mouse. And they're going to be getting their marching orders too.

Having added an extra verse to the incantation she used to raise the protective wards, she knows they haven't been tampered with. Once again her mom's spell book has come in handy. Upgrading the spell is especially pertinent now that Calico Jack is on the search for anything that might help her get back to *Garnet Cove*. Let's hope him being in possession of Zane's printer and Frankie's emailed files will have him backing off for now.

Despite knowing no-one has been on board, Frankie's pleased to see her phone is safe and sound on her bedside table where she left it. There's no way she's going to leave it behind again, not with Zane's houseboat having been broken into. At least if it's in her pocket and Calico Jack tries to get hold of it, she can beat the bejinkers out of him, Bruce Lee style. No, the only way she'd leave her phone behind is if Dex is at home.

Thanks to their telepathic connection, he's the best early warning system, ever.

"Be back soon." Frankie leaves Dex staring at his bowl of dog kibble and transports herself back to the *Annie*, arriving on the top deck rather than straight into the cabin. While others in the coven might think nothing of transporting themselves straight into someone's living room, Frankie was brought up differently. A quick rat-a-tat on the wheelhouse door and Stanley calls out for her to come on down. She finds him still examining the small chest she left behind.

"If it's okay with you, I'd like to take a closer look at the chest myself." Technically it's Frankie's property, so she doesn't need to ask for permission to retrieve it. Yet again, her mom's insistence on good manners stops her from simply grabbing it and disappearing.

"Yes, of course." Stanley picks it up and holds it out to her although she notices a smidge of reluctance on his part to hand it over. And it's this very thing that has prompted Frankie to come and retrieve the item. Without her knowing exactly what it is, she'd rather keep hold of it than turn it over to the coven leader, carte blanche.

"I promise I'll bring it back as soon as I've checked it out." Not allowing time for any further discussion on when this might be, Frankie transports herself and the chest back to the *Pearl*.

On returning to her cabin, Frankie finds Dex still sniffing his bowl as though the kibble sitting in the bottom will magically turn into muffins. There's less than a thin chance of that happening.

After stowing the small chest down the back of her soaking tub, she makes doubly sure it won't be found by hitting it with a concealment spell. She then picks up her phone and shoves it in the pocket of her jeans. "Come on buddy, let's go stretch our legs."

Frankie and Dex stride purposefully down the pier although Dex slows a little on passing *The Crate*. The way he's sniffing the air tells Frankie there are muffins left uneaten. Tough, he's going to have to wait because she's not joking when she threatens him with the diet biscuits. He's gained at least three pounds since they moved to the marina.

Frankie hasn't been brave enough to stand on the scales to find out how much damage she's done to herself courtesy of *Magic Beans*. It hadn't been a problem when she and Zane where in the middle of their martial arts training. These days while she's not exactly sedentary, she's moving nowhere near as much as she had been. And it's beginning to show.

While both she and Dex stare at the café longingly as they pass by, Frankie's on a mission and won't allow herself to be tempted. She's noticed *Bruce's Bits & Bytes* plenty of times but has never had need of the services on offer. Before now, that is.

Taking in the display in the front window she can tell the proprietor isn't interested in attracting foot traffic. The cobwebs that coat the museum quality computer sitting there are hardly likely to entice new customers unless they're after decorations for Halloween. It's the promise of large sized prints and not spooky party decorations that Frankie's more interested in.

She can't believe it's less than a couple of weeks until the holiday. It's one that's dear to Frankie's heart. Not because of its connection to magic, rather because it happens to be her birthday. She doubts there'll be much in the way of celebrations this year with it being her mom rather than Dex who always remembered her big day.

She's expecting it to pass without as much as a whimper with her not one to shout the fact from the rooftops. No, the only way there'll any fanfare this year will be if the coven likes to go all out on this most witching of nights and party like it's Halloween 1999.

She pushes the door open, expecting to hear a bell, or buzzer. But all is quiet.

Dex leans forward and sniffs the air. *"I can smell liniment, patchouli and WD40."*

"Hello?" Frankie inches her way into the gloomy interior of the shop, with Dex close on her heels. "Is there anyone here?" Frankie's at the point of leaving when she hears someone moving around in the furthest recesses.

"Be with ya in a mo'," comes a voice from somewhere down the back of the shop. Once again Dex is on the money, not that Frankie can smell anything. She's even careful not to breathe too deeply with the place containing more dust than is usual around computers.

Frankie's fully expecting an overweight guy in an ensemble of stretch knit to appear. She's therefore surprised by a tall man with a hippy vibe popping up from behind what looks like an explosion in a computer factory. None of the circuit boards and tangles of wire appear to belong together and none of them seem like they're capable of printing out the photos she's stored on the cloud. Never mind what the poster in the window says.

"How can I help ya?" The embroidery on his

shirt proclaims him as being Bruce and Frankie thinks it safe to assume he's the owner.

"I've got some photos I need printed." Frankie holds up her phone more out of habit than them actually being on there.

What follows is an exhibition of how little Frankie knows when it comes to cloud technology. If she still had the photos on her phone, it would be a simple matter of emailing them to him. Instead it takes five agonizing minutes of Bruce's help for her to find them and then download them to her smart phone. It's then straightforward enough and seconds after Frankie hits send on the email she's tapped into her phone, a ping announces its arrival on a computer somewhere down the back of the shop.

Frankie follows the IT hippy geek the length of the shop and is surprised on passing Mt Hard Drive to come upon a computer that is definitely state-of-the-art. The screen is big enough that you'd need to swivel your head to take everything in.

It's also the one piece of computer hardware in the shop not covered in a thick layer of dust. Some tinkering and Bruce has the first of Frankie's photos up on screen. It's the photo of the front of Calico Jack's amulet.

"Just a simple black and white print of that one, please."

The image on its way to print, Bruce brings up the photo of the back of the amulet and the process is repeated. It's when he brings up the first photo of the map that they stop talking, with both of them staring at the screen spell-bound.

"Wow, it almost looks 3D." Frankie leans in for a closer peek and it's as if her head is inside the map.

"What on earth did you take the photograph with?" Bruce examines his side of the screen as closely as Frankie's checking out hers. Rather than be fascinated as she is, he pulls back suddenly when he's not six inches away. "That is disturbing as hell."

"Oooh, can I see? Can I?" Dex already has his front paws on the vacant seat in front of the computer forcing Frankie to grab his collar to stop him from jumping up. If she can fit her whole head in the map, he'll be able to clamber inside completely.

"Are you going to be able to print it out?"

"We can but try." Bruce sits at his computer, keeping as far back from the screen as his long arms will allow. He brings up the print menu and punches in a whole stack of information that may as well be Greek to Frankie. She actually thinks Greek might be easier to understand.

A moment later and whirring starts on the far side of Mt Hard Drive. Bruce jumps up and inches his way around this potential avalanche, eager to check on progress. Frankie's keen on checking it out too. On seeing the size of the print slowly churning out of the printer she isn't so eager any more.

In Frankie's world ginormous equals horrendously expensive. Her funds are dwindling faster than cotton candy at a kid's birthday party, and this might be enough to see her and Dex living on noodles.

"How much is this going to cost?" Frankie's unable to stop her voice coming out squeaky.

"Relax would ya? The first one's on me. I just wanted to see if the printout is as weird as the photo is on screen."

The huge print isn't even half way through when it becomes obvious the map is sadly lacking on the 3D front. To Frankie it's a bit of a letdown.

When Bruce brings up her next photo of the map on screen, Frankie knows there might be a few noodles in her future. Even without comparing them side by side, she can see there are differences between the two photos. It shouldn't be possible, with the six photos having been taken in quick succession.

It was something Frankie had done to make sure at least one of them came out okay. She didn't expect them all to be different. One of them appears to be the same as that manifested by Calico Jack back on the island. The others are new to her. Is it that he can't see more than one layer? Is this why he's never found any reference to the runes on the island? Or had that all been a lie?

On leaving the shop, Frankie's credit card is feeling a little melted around the edges. She's also in possession of a tube of printouts that will need some serious examination on their return to the *Pearl*.

Rather than walk back down Pier 51 with the printouts in plain view, Frankie scurries from the computer shop and across to the far side of the carpark. Dex who's tagging along behind, yelps excitedly when he spots her unlocking the door of her beat-up Toyota.

"Thanks mom. We haven't been for a drive in ages."

Frankie hadn't planned ongoing for one now. All she wanted to do was get in, drop the seats back and transport the two of them from the car to the boat without being seen with the large maps.

On watching Dex bouncing with excitement, she knows she's going to have to do at least two laps of the block. This'll be the minimum to ensure any peace when she's back home. Possibly three laps for how long it's going to take to check all six printouts.

In the end it takes four laps before Dex, with his head hanging out the passenger window, runs out of drool. Even better is that on returning to the carpark Frankie finds a spot well away from Pier 51 and *Magic Beans*. No sooner has she yanked on the hand-brake, than she drops her seat back and transports the pair of them to the *Pearl*.

Before she's even had a chance to lay the maps out on the floor, Dex is on his back in the middle of her bed. Jinxed jack rabbits, he always snores when he lies like that. And with the speed at which the small pup can nod off, this will be sooner than she'd like.

Luckily she's got earplugs on hand and with these in place Frankie leans over the maps spread out around her. Next to them is a large Sherlock Holmes-style magnifying glass that will help her spot any finer details. A quick scan of each printout and she knows she's going to be making a lot of notes on the maps. While her main concern at the time had been cost, she's glad she opted for the matt paper rather than the glossy photo paper. If she's going to be living on noodles, she wants the good quality ones and not some cheap super-market brand.

Looking at each of the maps in turn, Frankie stills. She's spotted something that hadn't been visible either on screen, or on the 3D original at the jungle villa. It's something that could make all the difference to her search for her dad.

2

F rankie grabs the magnifying glass off the floor and leans forward to concentrate on the map legend at the bottom right of the first print-out. She knew it wasn't her imagination. Rather than being six items in the list, there are seven. As to what the seventh symbol relates to, this is going to require a visit to the island.

All she has to do is mark all the extra items on the first map. This way she'll have a master with everything showing. If she's lucky Calico Jack will print the maps out on Zane's printer at a much smaller size. This should have him missing the extra items that show up when the maps are printed out as large as Bruce has printed them for her.

It takes hours for Frankie to mark everything up to her satisfaction in what has amounted to a mega-size game of spot-the-difference. Most definitely the master map sitting in front of her has far more detail than either the original or Calico Jack's 3D rendering.

While knowing she's being paranoid, this doesn't stop Frankie taking half a dozen photographs of the composite map. She emails these to herself so there's a copy on the cloud. This way if the worst happens, and she loses her phone, or it's stolen, she'll still have a record of her work. And even better is that she knows how to retrieve them.

She's settling after all of this, when another thought occurs to her. Frankie grabs her phone and emails the composite map to Bruce at the computer shop asking him to store it somewhere safe. His being a *Normal*, Calico Jack won't think to check on the computer that's hiding behind Mt Hard Drive.

There's no way Calico Jack is going to get his hands on the copies, and especially not the fully marked up version. On hearing from Bruce that the file has been stored securely, Frankie deletes all reference to the map from her phone. She then takes the original up on deck.

A levitation spell soon has the map floating above the teak surface. A simple wiggle of her fingers and the large piece of paper is soon burning merrily. Following this all that's left is a haze of ash, which she sends flying with a wave of her hand.

It's then she remembers the other five maps and, wanting to leave nothing to chance, retrieves them and repeats the process. Not even Calico Jack is powerful enough to read them after this.

On her way back to her cabin, she pops into the bathroom and, after removing the concealment spell, collects the small cube from behind her bathtub. She places this on the Persian rug and sits on the ground next to it.

Taking up the magnifying glass, she wields it like Sherlock Holmes himself examining the cube inch by inch and turning it every which way in the process. This shows her that even the bottom of the chest has runes carved deep into its surface.

It's as though those who made it intended the base to be seen as much as the sides and top. In fact, after turning it around as much as she has, she's no longer sure what is top and what is bottom. Maybe it's not a chest after all? Could it be a solid cube? It's sure heavy enough.

Dex, who's woken from his nap, is lying with

his head hanging over the end of her bed, peering at the small cube. *"Why is it glowing?"*

Frankie sits up straight and looks at him. "What do you mean?"

"When you turned it, some grooves glowed." Dex wriggles forward until he's half hanging off the bed. *"Turn it again."*

Frankie does as instructed by her familiar, stopping the instant she hears his yelp of discovery. She checks the side of the cube that's facing toward him. There isn't any glow that she can see. She runs her hand over the surface to see if she can sense a change in surface. Again, there's nothing.

"Not that side, the other side."

Frankie flips it around so the side Dex is interested in is facing him. To her it looks as non-glowing as the side he's just seen.

"Oh, it's gone." Dex slides off the side of the bed and lands with a thump on the carpet. *"Turn it again."*

Frankie does, and again Dex confirms he sees something.

"Are you sure about that?" Half her attention on the little Jack Russell and half on the cube, means it takes longer than it should to register she can see something too. While not visible when she looks directly at it, there's definitely a faint glow when it's viewed on an angle.

Sure enough, looking at one of the surfaces from an acute angle, she can see a definite glow from a couple of the groves that form the runes. She checks the next side. Again there's nothing. The same happens with the other four sides. Hmmm, so it's only glowing on one side of the cube.

"Dex can you put your paw on this side for me?" Him in place, Frankie jumps up and goes into the bathroom where she grabs a Band-Aid from the cabinet over the sink. "This'll work." Back on the rug, she opens the plaster and sticks this to the side with the glowing grooves. Now even if the runes stop glowing, she'll still know which side is the right side.

Frankie leans up and grabs her handbag off the top of the dresser. A quick search in her wallet and she holds up a quarter. She slides this into one of the grooves emitting light. Absolutely nothing happens. She tries sliding the coin back and forth. Again nothing happens, apart from the coin getting stuck. "Broomsticks!" Try as she might she's unable to free the coin. That is until she summons a pair of pliers from an auto repair shop nearby. By using these she's able to yank the quarter free.

"Well, that was a bust." Frankie drops the coin back into the side pouch of her bag and shoves it behind her. "I'm going to need to have a lie down and think about this."

Frankie doesn't bother with her bed while pondering the riddle of how to access the glowing interior of the cube. Instead she lies back on the Persian rug and uses the small cube like a geisha pillow. While thinking on her current quandary she fiddles with her amulet before dropping it and allowing it to swing around on the chain and hang behind her neck.

Initially nothing happens.

"Wow, that's cool." Dex has his head shoved in the gap under her neck, sniffing excitedly at the cube.

Frankie knows he must be witnessing a reaction between the cube and her amulet and worries if she moves that she'll throw things out alignment. "What's happening?"

"It's glowing really bright now."

"The runes or the cube itself?"

"The runes. And your amulet too."

Frankie reaches around behind her neck and takes hold of the amulet. Dex gives her directions allowing her to move the charm toward the groove that's glowing enough to have it seem like her hair is on fire. At least according to Dex, this is.

Frankie knows she's achieved her goal when the clasp on the chain that holds the amulet around her neck, pops open. This isn't something that shouldn't have been able to happen. Not with the killer hex Calico Jack placed on it. According to him the only way the chain could be removed was if her head was removed in the process. Something he'd shared after the fact.

Was it that he'd hexed the chain as strongly as he did in order to make sure Frankie never removed it, even willingly? Frankie wouldn't put it past him.

Frankie flips over onto her stomach and picks up her amulet. She tentatively slides this into the groove that's glowing brighter than any of the others. Nothing happens other than the amulet being as jammed as the coin had been earlier. "Well, that's a letdown."

"Perhaps the chain needs to be still around your neck?"

While this might be Jack Russell logic, Frankie is willing to try anything. Rolling over onto her back, Frankie wriggles until she's got her head over the top of the cube. She reaches around behind her neck and grabbing both ends of the chain does the clasp up at the front of her throat.

The reaction is immediate, and intense. This time, rather than be flooded with power, Frankie is positively overwhelmed. It's not so much that she feels like something has been released inside her but rather that she's been imbued with power held by the cube itself. It's the nature of the power that has her worried. One thing she does know, even with her limited experience, is that this is definitely not witchy power.

Whatever it is, the levels swirling through her body are such that everything on the *Pearl* vibrates and Dex levitates above the carpet. He even manages some doggie paddle action before settling back down again.

Frankie goes to sit up, but she's got a problem. Not only will the clasp not release, neither will the amulet come free of the groove in the cube. And while the cube might be small, it's not tiny enough to wear on a chain. She'd look like she had a cinder block hanging around her neck, for goodness' sake.

"Oh heck!"

Dex who's lying on his back on the carpet next to her rolls over. *"What's wrong?"*

Frankie explains her predicament. Not that she

thinks that Dex, lacking opposable thumbs will be of any help to her.

"Do you want me to press the red button with my nose?"

Frankie turns her head as far as she's able, and peers at him. "What red button?"

"The one that's on the side of the little box."

Frankie isn't sure she wants him pushing any red buttons. Red buttons usually mean a big old kaboom. If it was a green button she'd be fine with him pushing it. "Do you want to check the other sides and see if you can't find a green button?"

He's busy sniffing around her head when Zane pops into focus in her cabin.

"What in Hades did you just do?"

"What do you mean, what did I do?" What is it with him thinking she's responsible for every weird occurrence on the marina? Not willing to reveal she's guilty this time and stuck where she is, Frankie lies back, making out she's having a re-laxing afternoon.

She even thinks she's succeeding until she sees Zane frown. Dex has given up his exploration of the small cube, meaning Frankie is going to need Zane's help to get out of this jam. And for that she's going to have to fess up that she is re-sponsible.

"I, ah, managed to unlock the cube, and..."

Zane hunkers down next to, leaning forward so he can examine the cube as closely as she and Dex have already done. "I see you got the amulet into one of the runes. Was that what released that huge surge of power we all felt?"

Frankie had been wondering about this. What she felt on the *Pearl* had been strong. It's not much of a stretch to grasp others in the coven might have picked up on it.

"Yeah, but that didn't happen until I undid the clasp on the chain."

"And how exactly did you get the clasp undone? I thought Calico Jack made it that you couldn't get that off no matter how hard you tried?" Frankie goes through everything from start to finish. She leaves out no detail until Zane knows as much about what's happened as she does herself. Like her, he's in the *'don't push the red button'* camp with his own experience of red buttons not having been good.

The solution he comes up with is a very human one of using bolt cutters on the chain. Due to its sentimental value, this isn't something Frankie wants to try, preferring to push the red button over that. Zane pacing backward and forward in thought, Frankie casually puts her hand

behind her head and groping around feels for anything like a button.

She knows she's found the right spot, not because of any protuberances, rather because of the
heat being generated. Her finger on the right spot,
she throws a wall of protection up around herself
Zane, Dex and even the *Pearl*.

She then presses the button.

And waits.

3

The first thing to happen is the cube spitting out her amulet. It hits Frankie in the back of her neck hard enough that she suspects there'll be a bruise. The second thing is that she levitates about a foot off the ground, all while vibrating hard enough to have her teeth rattling. Only when she's back down on the Persian rug is Frankie brave enough to open her eyes.

A quick check of Dex shows him to have come through whatever it was unscathed.

Zane looks to be in the same state. Not that he appears happy about it. "What on earth, were you thinking?"

"Relax would you? I threw up wards!" Frankie scrambles to her feet and picks up the cube. Anything's better than groveling around on the carpet at his feet.

Turing her back on him, Frankie re-examines the small cube. Even looking carefully at the side with the plaster at an acute angle, she can see no longer see a glow. It's something that's confirmed by Dex. Frankie's hoping if she ignores Zane long enough he'll eventually leave. But her hope is in vain. As if he wasn't enough to deal with, Stanley then arrives. One look at his face and Frankie puts the cube down on the end of her bed. Best to have both hands free if things go pear-shaped.

"What in the name of all that is magical just happened?" Frankie's a little peeved he's looking at her rather than Zane or Dex.

As if reading her body language of crossed arms and mutinous glare, Zane explains everything to Stanley. Frankie has to admit that hearing him say it out loud, her pushing the red button does come across as a tad dangerous. Not that it had felt like this to her at the time. Deep down, she knew she was going to be okay. However, she couldn't say how she knew this.

Stanley's still shaking his head in disbelief, when Frankie holds her hand up. "Have I got my full powers back now?" The hex her mom placed on her all those years ago not having been officially removed, Frankie isn't sure. To offset this, there's the power that swamped her when the amulet went into the groove. Add to that the dose she'd received on pushing the red button, and she should be up to snuff.

In response to her request, Stanley explores her aura as he's done previously. What hasn't happened before is him yanking his hands back as though he's been burnt.

Frankie runs her hands over her body, expecting to find it burning hot. On the contrary, her skin feels cool to the touch. "What?"

Stanley frowns, looking to be concentrating on finding the right words. He takes long enough that Zane straightens and pushes away from the dresser. "Is it something we should be concerned about?"

"I haven't felt that type of energy in a long time."

Talk about your answer when you don't want to give an answer. Frankie stares hard at Stanley before speaking. "And..." He still hasn't responded when she hits him with more questions. "Bad energy? Good energy? Evil? Alien?"

"It's not bad, as such."

Frankie's able to sense a 'but' hanging in the

air like a rabid bat waiting to sink its pointy little teeth into her.

"I'll need to research this." Without giving Zane or Frankie a chance to ask anything further, the coven leader disappears.

Not that Frankie's going to let him get away that easily. Without thinking, she transports herself to the main cabin of the tugboat *Annie* and to heck with bad manners. She expects to find Stanley buried in *The Lore of Crafte* as if searching for a really good muffin recipe. Instead she finds the cabin empty. There's no sign of Stanley or the book, with even Jojo the Siamese missing from her spot on the sofa. Perhaps the largest thing to be missing is the terrarium, presumably with George and Gwen still in residence

She's looking down at the sideboard that had once held the large glass container, when Zane appears in the cabin behind her. "Hmmm, guess this means I'm in charge."

Frankie swings to face him. "What do you mean?"

"Stanley's off visiting the Council, that puts me in charge."

The council? Is he talking a capital C or a lower case c?

Without a formal induction into the coven,

Frankie's in the dark about the politics of the witching community as a whole. If the witchy council is anything like any other council she's had to deal with, there'll be a lot of red tape and paperwork. Stanley could be gone for weeks. It's a worry she voices to Zane although he doesn't appear as concerned as she is.

Frankie isn't sure where this leaves her when it comes to her newly bolstered powers. Surely she's packing enough heat she can go looking for Mimi Merriweather? And with Zane tied up looking after the coven, this means she and Dex won't have as much trouble slipping away. The first thing Frankie has to work on is getting herself back to the island and she's not going to do that hanging around on the *Annie*.

"Well, I guess until Stanley comes back there's nothing else we can do." To avoid any cross-examination by Zane, Frankie zaps herself back to the *Pearl*, grabs Dex and then transports the pair of them straight to *Magic Beans*.

Frankie is surprised that even though her coffee order today is different, Mac is already busy making the two coffees and has bagged up the right number of muffins. How he does this is anyone's guess, but it does come in handy.

Five minutes later and Frankie leaves the cafe

holding onto two takeaway cups of the best coffee in Seattle. Unfortunately she's not wearing her hoodie and so Dex trots along behind her, the top of the muffin bag held firmly in his teeth. It's something Frankie will need to sort fast, with his drool already turning the brown paper bag dark.

This time on entering *Bruce's Bits & Bytes* she doesn't bother announcing herself. Instead she wends her way through the heaps of computer parts with Dex close behind. Sure enough on rounding the large pile of spares at the end of the shop she finds Bruce. He's at his desk playing what she imagines is some online computer game.

Frankie puts the coffees down on the desk beside his keyboard and grabs the muffin bag off Dex but her hopes of saving the paper bag have been in vain. There's no way she can hand the muffins over to Bruce now. While she waits for the hippy geek to take a break from the game, Frankie feeds small pieces of muffin to a very grateful Dex. It takes longer than she's expecting for the game to be over. Dex has finished one of his muffins and she's finished her coffee before he reaches the next level and puts the game on pause. Only after he's taken his first mouthful of coffee does she truly have is attention.

"Where are on earth," he takes another sip,

"did you get this," he has another sip, "amazing coffee?"

Magic Beans being a café of the magical variety, Frankie's unable to tell him. Even if she did, he'd never find the place. She hadn't thought it through when she bought the coffee from there. "I, I've got a coffee machine at home. My parents used to own a cafe." On seeing him looking at the takeaway cup with its plastic lid, she adds. "I've still got a stack of cups I'm working through." She isn't sure where these lies are coming from. Thankfully they seem to assuage Bruce's curiosity.

It's not until he's sucked the takeaway cup dry and removed the lid and scooped out any remaining foam using his finger, that Bruce is any good to her.

"I need your help with something."

"You can have anything you want after bringing me a coffee like that."

Frankie explains she'd like to know more about the island where the photos of the maps were taken. "Can you find that out from the photo itself?" She's read somewhere that it's possible.

"So long as the GPS on your phone was switched on when the photo was taken, then yeah, for sure."

While not a complete technophobe, there are a

few holes in Frankie's knowledge of all the functionality of her smart phone. "I'm not sure. We'll need to see."

Lucky for Frankie, Bruce still has the images on the desktop of his computer. Even luckier is that it would appear Frankie did have the GPS switched on. A short lecture from Bruce that includes warnings about people tracking you down and all sorts of tinfoil hat theories, this function is disabled.

Even though it's unlikely anyone in the witching community would track her down using this technology, she wouldn't put anything past the Garnets. On seeing how easily Bruce finds out where the photo was taken, Frankie's thinking of adding tinfoil to her shopping list.

The co-ordinates are put into Google Earth and soon Frankie has a bird's-eye view of *Garnet Cove*. Bruce hits the zoom button and Frankie suffers from a small dose of vertigo as they plummet toward the island from satellite height. They keep going until Frankie is even able to make out people sunbathing on the beach. She's especially glad she's turned the GPS function off on her phone. Talk about big brother.

"Are you able to pull back slightly so I can see exactly where it is?"

"Didn't you take the photos?"

"I ah, no. My old phone was stolen and I'm trying to track down where it is."

Bruce looks at her strangely before doing as she's asked. He pulls back giving her an idea of where *Garnet Cove* sits in relation to better-known locations.

Bruce taps the screen with the eraser end of a pencil. "The closest airport is probably going to be on Bermuda."

It's Bruce zooming back out in Google Earth that allows Frankie to see exactly how smack bang in the middle of the Bermuda Triangle, the island really is. It sort of makes sense when she thinks about it.

Frankie leaves with thanks and promises of more coffee, and she and Dex are soon aboard the *Pearl*. Not that they're there for long. She takes only as long as she needs to disguise her and Dex so they won't be recognized if any of the guards happen to see them.

Blonde in nature
and blonde in hue
Weave your magic,
transform these two.
Make them stand out

from the crowd
Make them brash and
make them loud.

Their outfits are intended to be hideous enough to allow them to blend in with other visitors to the resort. Better this than acting like they're up to no good. Frankie then grabs the small printout of the composite map that Bruce gave her. Unlike the others, this one folds down small enough she can shove it in her bra. Luckily the pineapple print of her sun frock is busy enough that any sharp corners will be missed.

She's smoothing down the front of the bright green and yellow dress — hidden in plain sight — when there's a howl of anguish from the bathroom.

Blast, she's been hoping to avoid this.

"I can't go outside looking like this."

The indignation displayed by Dex's at her having turned him into a poodle is almost as funny as the over-the-top Lion Clip she's hit him with. Okay so maybe she shouldn't have turned his fur a soft green to match her dress.

"Are any of the guards we ran into before going to recognize you?"

Dex continues to stare at himself in the bathroom mirror in horror. He doesn't seem to be convinced.

"Think about it," Frankie fluffs the riot of blonde curls that sits atop her head in a messy bun. "If anyone sees us, we can be completely obnoxious as part of our cover." She's deliberately lumped herself in with him in hopes of comradery.

On seeing the sideways peek he gives her, she knows she's hit on something he can appreciate. It's something that appeals to his naughty side, although she shouldn't encourage his sometimes bad behavior. The Goddess knows he doesn't need it.

Frankie takes one last glimpse at Google Earth on her phone. She turns it off and stuffs it along with her wand into a specially designed pocket inside the dress. On hearing footsteps out on the dock she doesn't stop to think. She clicks her fingers and on cue Dex jumps into arms.

They arrive at the island without any hangers on. Phew, she got away with it.

Rather than manifest them into the middle of the resort, Frankie and Dex arrive at the very end of the beach. They're behind some rocks Frankie has seen on Google Earth. This position is also closest to the mysterious seventh rune.

A quick peek over the top of the rocks and Frankie is surprised to see no-one on the beach. Not only that but the dock's empty, with the high-end launches that had been there on her earlier visits, no longer tied up. Maybe the place is unable to survive without George Garnet around to run it? Well, that's just tough. If Frankie has any say in the matter, he's never returning to the island.

Not wanting to dwell on the man's possibly having something to do with the death of her mom, Frankie turns away from the crystal blue water and heads into the jungle. The one concession she's made with her outfit is that she's wearing sneakers. To be fair, they're fashionable gold sneakers, but they're still sturdy enough to tackle the jungle. Luckily for the pair of them after an initial wall of palm leaves, it's fairly easy going. Even better is that Frankie comes upon the site of the seventh rune after ten minutes of walking. At least she thinks this is the right spot.

While the cliff is marked on the map as a small squiggle, here it's monstrously large, with her and Dex feeling very small by comparison. The trees that stand sentinel nearby are also huge and don't look to be native to the island. If Frankie was to guess, she'd say they were redwoods with their girth putting them at several hundred years old.

On looking at the nearest trunk, Frankie sees something that's out of the ordinary in this tranquil setting.

Is that a heart? She moves closer and her suspicions are confirmed. Inside the carved heart shape are the initials CJ and AB. Huh, so much for Calico Jack not being able to find any reference to the runes on the island. Not that him lying through his teeth should altogether surprise Frankie. It's then she realizes she can see something glistening in the initials. A closer look shows it to be tree sap. The carving is still fresh.

Frankie peers into the jungle beyond, looking for any sign of her missing relatives. She quiets her breathing and even tells Dex to do the same. She can't hear anything except the occasional squawk of a parrot.

Confident they're on their own and with the small map stuffed safely back in her bra, they inch their way along the wall of granite, searching high and low for the seventh rune. If she hadn't been looking, she never would have found the graphic. Unlike the granite cliff face, the rune is small. Unfortunately it's also high up. So high, Frankie has to clamber up on a large boulder in order to be able to examine it in detail.

No sooner has she steadied herself atop the

boulder than her amulet lights up. A beam of light shoots out of the charm, locking onto the carved symbol like a heat-seeking missile. On hearing the rocks in front of her grating, Frankie wastes no time getting back down to the jungle floor. Not wanting to take her eyes off events in front of her, Frankie doesn't look at Dex when she speaks to him. "Are you seeing, what I'm seeing?"

"Yeah, I am." Rather than displaying his usual inquisitive nature, Dex is backing up.

Frankie matches him pace for pace, not liking the fissure in front of them splitting wider with each groan of the rock. From something narrow enough she wouldn't risk putting her hand inside, it's wide enough for her and Dex to walk through side-by-side.

She's even thinking about doing so until she sees something walking toward them through the gap in the rock. Scratch that. This isn't so much a something as a plain old 'thing' with Frankie scrambling for a description she can give to her grandchildren.

That's if she ever gets to have them.

4

Frankie tries moving her feet. They're rooted to the ground. The closer the thing gets to her, the more horrified she becomes. Her brain scrambles for a term that describes what it is she's seeing. What comes up is a jumbled scattering of thoughts.

Her best description would be that it's like somebody has been hunting and cut all the carcasses into little bits and pieces. They've then stitched them back together in the shape of a human, complete with human hands, although Frankie suspects this exception is purely down to opposable thumbs. This thing's a 'bitzer' in the true sense of the word.

"Um, aren't you going to do something?" So conversational is Dex's tone Frankie doesn't immediately realize he's freaking out as much as she is. *"Can you stop it getting any closer?"*

This she can do. Thanks to her new powers Frankie doesn't even need to think about an incantation. It's a good thing too, with her cognitive abilities currently about as much use as cream-style corn. Simply pointing at the thing is enough of a challenge. Even though she's shaking in her sneakers, she manages this small task with the thing freezing instantly. Only when she's sure it's not going to move does Frankie step forward in order to examine it. Dex stays exactly where he is.

Frankie walks around the thing, examining it in minute detail. It's even uglier this close-up and there's an awful smell that reminds her of boiled cabbage and dog food. Not a good combination in anyone's cookbook. She reaches out and tentatively strokes the fur that covers the chest of the abomination. On hearing a low growl she jumps back, nearly falling over.

"Are you going to send it back?"

Once again Dex is the voice of reason. The merest flick of her wrist and Frankie sends the beast back through the crevasse in the rock. No sooner has it disappeared into the crevasse than her amulet lights up again and the rock slams shut. It's the granite equivalent of automatic doors. Unsure if this is going be enough to keep the feral jigsaw where it is, Frankie wastes no time transporting herself and Dex back to Zane's place.

She'd contemplated going home to the *Pearl* before discounting that. If the thing can follow her home, the last thing she needs is to be alone. While this might sound selfish, she prefers having someone of Zane's capabilities at her side to greet any unwelcome guests.

This doesn't work out according to plan because rather than pop into focus in the middle of Zane's great room she finds herself outside and staring at that ugly octopus door knocker of his. This can mean one thing, and it's that Zane isn't home. Otherwise she would have been able to transport them inside.

"Maybe he's at Stanley's place seeing as he's in charge?"

Frankie shakes her head. "Hmmm, I'm not sure about that? Can you imagine Zane living on the *Annie* rather than at his own place?" The coven leader's tugboat is the antithesis of Zane's sleek, modern houseboat, and Frankie can't see him being keen on moving in.

Without knowing if the 'thing' she saw earlier

will be able to track them down, Frankie hurries across the pier and down the side dock to the door of *The Crate*. A quick knock on the sliding glass door and Magda slides it open. "Yes?"

It's Magda looking at her and Dex like she's never laid eyes on them that reminds Frankie they're still in disguise. She's got a choice. She can either admit she's been sneaking around on the island incognito, or pretend she's someone else. In the end she doesn't like the idea of telling lies to Magda. The vamp is the closest thing she's had to a friend in years and she's not about to risk that. A quick wave of her wand, and she and Dex are back looking like themselves.

"You 'ave mastered the technique so very well. I could not even sense your energy."

"Really?" Frankie's surprised. She thought she'd simply changed their outside appearance as usual. To change their very energy is transformation at a whole new level. For sure her disguises in the past have been rudimentary at best and blimmin' useless at worst. They'd consist of the same basic Frankie, with different colored hair or she's in a dress rather than her usual jeans and t-shirt or hoodie. It looks as though her new powers are far more impressive than anything she's had access to so far in life.

"What 'ave you been up to?"

Frankie has a quick look over her shoulder before turning back to Magda. "Can we talk about this inside?"

"Of course, I will make the coffee."

Dex doesn't need to be asked twice. Him knowing there will more than likely be muffins on offer with the coffee, he squeezes between the two women before they've had a chance to move. On entering the shipping container, Frankie's once again surprised at how different the inside of *The Crate* is with Magda in residence.

For someone who's just here on holiday her friend sure knows how to make herself at home. The bohemian charm is even starting to work its magic on Frankie. Perhaps she'll get Magda to help her with some interior decoration over on the *Pearl* before the vamp heads home to Europe. Not that she's said anything about leaving.

Over coffee Frankie comes clean on what she and Dex have been up to and what they discovered on the island.

"You need to talk to Stanley or Zane about this. I 'ave an idea what it is, this thing you 'ave found. I could be wrong. They are very rare in this realm. So very rare."

Despite a lot of prodding from Frankie, Magda

isn't forthcoming with any more information than this, continuing to fob her off. "You must ask Stanley or Zane if you want to know more."

"I would, except Stanley's gone to visit some council and Zane isn't at home."

"Some council, or THE Council?"

"I'm not sure. Zane wouldn't tell me anything about it. Is it bad?"

Rather than respond in words, Magda gives one of those very European shrugs of hers. At least Frankie is familiar enough with it to understand what it means in general terms. This also means she still has no idea whether it's a good or bad thing that Stanley has shot off to confer with the Council.

They're finishing up their coffees when Frankie tries to get Magda to look at her crystal ball again. Whereas in the past the European beauty has been eager to look into Frankie's future, she's strangely reticent. There being nothing else to keep her there, Frankie and Dex are soon on their way. Rather than go home to the *Pearl*, Frankie heads in the direction of the *Annie*. She wants to check if, against all odds, Zane is in residence there while he's in charge.

She's therefore surprised on knocking on the door of the wheelhouse at the tugboat, that it's

Stanley who calls out to her to come below. His visit to the Council being over this quickly can either be a good, or very bad, thing. Frankie's having second thoughts about coming clean to the coven leader.

By visiting the island she's gone against his instructions not to go after Mimi Merriweather without full powers. Okay, so they might not be *her* powers but they're powers she can use, so surely that counts as something?

Rather than clamber down the metal ladder, Frankie transports herself and Dex to the cabin below. This is also a lot easier than trying to get Dex down the ladder. It takes the merest glance to see that as well as the coven leader, Jojo the Siamese and the terrarium are back too.

Frankie peers at the ferns that crowd the end of the glass enclosure closest to her. For a second she worries the lizard once known as George Garnet is missing. Then she spots the Gecko hiding in the foliage. "I'm glad he's back. I still need to get information out of him as to who was responsible for the death of my mom."

She's ready to tap the glass to get lizard George's attention when Stanley walks over to her and sniffs deeply. "Frankie, what have you done?"

Rather than go on the defensive, Frankie opts

to go on the attack. "You said when I had my full powers that I could go in search of Mimi Merriweather. You said it! I've got them, so I went."

"I said when you had YOUR full powers that you could go in search of my demon of an ex-wife. The powers you're currently in possession of are not yours and you have no idea what the consequences of you using them will be."

"Nothing so far." On seeing the expression on Stanley's face Frankie would give anything to take those three words back.

"Ruh roh, someone is in trouble."

Frankie looks down at Dex. *"If I am, then so are you, so stop looking so smug."*

Stanley marches to the far end of the cabin and back before stopping directly in front of her. "I can tell you one consequence of you having disobeyed a direct order from your coven leader. You will be stripped of your powers for two weeks. I'd like you to hand your wand over now."

Gone is the timid little man Frankie has come to know, replaced by someone who looks as though he won't give an inch. She still can't work out how she's supposed to respond to this threat, when he waves his hand at her. Next thing she knows, he's holding her mom's wand. He then has the gall to use it to take her powers away from her.

Stripped of power
and mute of spell
Let this lesson
help you quell
your need to flaunt
these rules of ours
as only then you'll
have your powers.

Encased in a pearlescent cloud, Frankie can feel a sneeze threatening. Only pinching her nose with her fingers stops it. She can't believe it. She's just got some powers and here they are being taken away from her. Not that she feels any different.

"I'd like my mom's wand back please." Frankie holds her hand out to reinforce her request. Not that it does any good, with Stanley throwing the wand up in the air it and disappearing in a shower of sparks.

It's been a long time since Frankie has been this angry, and she worries that she could do the small man in front of her real harm. Even without her magic, she's a power to be reckoned with. The drive to put him in a headlock is so overwhelming that she knows if she doesn't leave soon she won't be held responsible for her actions.

"Can you please send Dex back to the *Pearl* as I can't carry him up the ladder?" Frankie's tone is clipped, with her having to force the words out. While her preference is let Stanley know what she thinks of him, she knows no good will come of it.

Stanley having transported Dex back to the schooner for Frankie, she can see no reason to stay. She's walking toward the ladder when she feels tingling between her shoulder blades, followed by Stanley shouting the word, "Immobilis". Frankie stops dead. Not because his spell has worked, more that she wants him to think it has.

She stays exactly where she is. She doesn't turn. She doesn't as much as twitch. Part of her would be shocked into stillness anyway purely by the fact the coven leader has hit her with a spell from behind. Rather underhanded in Frankie's mind.

"Where did you go, Frankie?"

Not sure if the immobilis spell is able to rob her of her speech, she responds telepathically. *"The island."*

"And did you see anything there that I should know about?"

Frankie considers keeping quiet about what she's seen. However, Magda had been insistent she let Zane or Stanley know everything. And so she does.

On her describing the 'thing' to him, he admits he knows what it is.

"If I lift the immobilis spell, can you promise me, you won't run away?"

Even though this is exactly what she wants to do, Frankie reluctantly agrees to stay on the *Annie*, not least because she wants to know what that thing is. With knowledge being power at least she'll know what she's up against on her return to the island.

Frankie waits for a couple of seconds after Stanley lifts the spell he thinks is keeping her frozen. She doesn't want to move too soon and let him know the spell has failed. As to why that is, this is a puzzle for another day.

Frankie sits next to him on the sofa and watches Stanley flick through *The Lore of Crafte* that was still on the coffee table from the previous day. The pages are slammed open, and Frankie leans forward. Yup, the illustration is every bit as ugly as the thing she saw on the island. Stitch that, the thing on the island had been even uglier. Perhaps that was the smell. Even now she can't rid her nostrils of the revolting combination.

"Is this what you saw?"

"Pretty much."

Stanley taps the page before speaking. "At least we know how it is that Mimi is able to warp time as she does. It would appear I've underestimated my ex-wife."

Sensing a juicy bit of gossip, Frankie turns in his seat to face him. "How so?"

It turns out the Werealls — the ugly combo creatures — are the guardians of the ominously named *All Hallows Keep*. For Mimi Merriweather to have thrown her lot in with this sub-species apparently beggars belief. "She must have something on one of them for them to even contemplate speaking to the evil woman let alone allowing her to use the powers of the *Keep*."

"If she's involved with the Werealls as well as the Garnet family, might that be where my dad is being held?"

Stanley continues to stare at the open pages in front of them rather than answer Frankie. If she was a betting woman, she'd say he's coming up with a plausible lie. She's therefore surprised when he turns toward her, his eyes full of compassion. "Yes, it might well be. It would certainly explain why it was that Magda couldn't pick up on your father."

"How so?"

"Because *All Hallows Keep* exists in neither time, nor space. It's where we send those prisoners that are beyond redemption."

"But my dad wasn't beyond redemption. From what my mum tells me he was a good man. There's no way he should be locked up somewhere like that." Frankie isn't aware of her agitation until Stanley squeezes her shoulder reassuringly.

"If he is, we'll get him out. You having found the portal to the *Keep*, means the hard part is over."

"Zane is gonna flip when he hears about this."

"Yes, about Zane, he's had to leave to deal with something."

"Family stuff?" Frankie knows she's being nosy. She and Zane are only starting to open up to each other. For him to up sticks — ah make that sea-weed — and scamper off is not ideal.

Stanley's cagey about what exactly Zane is off doing, which has Frankie imagining all sorts of scenarios, with none of them great. Her brain is flooded with more and more outrageous ideas, with her pulling on her new powers to help her. She's done so unconsciously and hopes Stanley hasn't sensed anything. "He's gone after Calico Jack, hasn't he?"

Stanley reluctantly confirms this is true.

"But he's my relation. I should be the one to go after the thieving so-and-so!" Never mind that Calico Jack has stolen Zane's printer, there's the issue of him taking the original treasure map. By taking it he more than likely hoped to stop Frankie from returning to the island. Thank the Goddess her GPS was on when she took the photos of the map. But he wasn't to know that. The main aim of her grandparents would be making it impossible for her to return.

Frankie is under no illusions about her relatives, she knows full well this wasn't to protect her, but rather to protect them. It also points to there being a lot more loot buried on the island. And loot that Calico Jack and Anne want to dig up at their leisure without her around.

The island seemingly the key to everything from regaining her powers to finding her dad, for them to stop her from returning is not to be borne. She pushes Stanley until he reluctantly admits that Zane could be in danger because Calico Jack is the strongest warlock he's ever met.

"Even stronger than you?" Frankie doubts it. However, it's something that Stanley confirms, with Frankie's relative apparently having three times the power of the coven leader.

"Three times?!"

"While you're relieved of your powers, you should take the opportunity to study *All Hallows Keep* and the Werealls."

Frankie is shocked. She's being given home-work? Still, if she's pretending she's powerless, she needs to play along. Frankie pulls her phone out the pocket of her jeans. She then sets about taking photos of the pages and pages of information about *All Hallows Keep* and its guardians the Were-alls. She's done this on instinct with her doubting the coven will allow her to take the hefty book home. Neither does she want to spend time reading the actual pages on the *Annie* like she's on detention. Pity, because she'll bet there are a lot of juicy bits and pieces between those covers.

Frankie takes a photo of each page, starting at the back of the section on *All Hallows Keep* and working her way to the front. This way they'll read in the right direction on her phone. From the few snippets she skim reads about the *Keep*, being turned into a lizard and kept in a nice warm ter-rarium doesn't seem so bad, after all. It's better than being stripped of your powers and locked up in the supernatural equivalent of Alcatraz.

Her poor dad. What shape is he going to be in after being incarcerated in this sort of hell for over twenty years? It doesn't bear contemplation. She'd have lost her marbles by now, for sure.

5

Back on the *Pearl*, Frankie reads about *All Hallows Keep* over and over until the words are swimming on the small screen of her smart phone. It's a nuisance Zane's printer is missing in action as the old fashion script would be much easier to read if she could print the photos out.

She swipes back through the series of photos again. There's something she's missing. How can it be that the Garnets who are human through-and-through are mixed up with this? As tempting as it is to head over to the computer shop and get Bruce to print everything out, there are two things stopping her. He'll start to get suspicious about the strange images and she'll be forced to eat supermarket noodles in order to pay for all the printouts.

Could *All Hallows Keep* be where the Garnets have stashed all their business foes? Not killed off, simply held in a parallel universe like indentured servants. It would make sense if you had this many business leaders in one place that they'd be able to rule the stock-market plus a lot of other markets.

But what of the witches and warlocks held there. What are they being used for? No longer in possession of their powers, they're nothing more than humans with a great sense of style. Frankie drops her phone on the bedside table and turns toward Dex. "If you had lots and lots of power, what would you do?"

He rolls from his back onto his side and faces her. She can see the machinations have already begun. It doesn't take long before she has the answer she's been expecting.

"I'd be bad, very bad. Who'd stop me?" He gets to his feet and assumes his attack pose. *"I'd be invincible!"*

"Yeah, yeah, steady on there, Attila the Hound."

Frankie tugs on one of his ears affectionately. While he might have gone overboard in his response, it's what Frankie's been thinking too. Not that she'd be bad, rather that the powerful end up this way. What was the saying about power corrupting? That's right 'Absolute power corrupts absolutely'. It stands to reason the magical folk imprisoned at the *Keep* are there because they're bad. Ergo, they're also powerful. Or they were until those powers were siphoned off.

This leads onto why her dad is locked up despite being one of the good guys. Calico Jack said she was the weakest Bonny in two hundred years. On hearing about Calico Jack's own levels of power, it doesn't take a genius to understand members of the Bonny family would be the obvious target for someone after this sort of power.

And who'd want that sort of power?

"That's it!"

"What?" Dex looks around the cabin trying to pinpoint exactly what 'it' is. Not that he's alarmed enough to resume his attack pose.

"No. Think about it. If they can take the prisoners powers away, there must be some way of giving them back on their release. That's if they ever release anyone." The question Frankie wants an answer to is whether these powers being given to someone else instead?

Mindful of this, she picks up her phone again. Switching to landscape mode goes some way toward making the words on the page easier to read. Also with her looking for reference to one thing she skims the pages rather than reads them line-by-line.

She's getting towards the end when she finds what it is she's looking for. There's reference to the *Syphonia*. From the way it's worded, Frankie gets the impression this thing holds the key to the powers taken from inmates.

She's about to get in touch with Stanley to confirm her suspicions, but decides it can wait. Comfortable where she is, she finishes skimming all the pages before getting up and going to visit the coven leader.

There are three more things in the final pages that jump out and all of them are incantations. The first is designed to open the fissure in the rock face. Frankie doesn't need to remember this with her amulet taking care of that. The second and third are far more interesting. The second allows the person who says the words to put *All Hallows Keep* in stasis while the third can unfreeze the realm. That's if they're in possession of enough power.

Frankie isn't sure why, but she gets that remembering the second incantation is important. She zooms in on the passage and takes a screenshot. She then skims the rest of the pages, not finding anything else of note. Well, other than a few horror stories about some inmates.

Frankie hops off the bed and turns to Dex. "I'm going back down to Stanley's. Do you want to come?" While her preference would be to discuss her theory with Zane, Stanley will have to do. Dex's lack of action on the getting up front tells her more clearly than words that he's going to stay right where he is.

Frankie walks down the pier like a *Normal*, saying hello to a few members of the coven who are sunning themselves in the autumnal rays. Even Magda is sitting outside in a deck chair at *The Crate*, proving she's like no other vampire. The weather being unseasonably warm as it is, Frankie hasn't bothered with shoes and is padding down the wooden decking in bare feet.

Maybe it's this that allows her to step up onto the deck of the *Annie* undetected. She hears Stanley talking through the open door to the wheelhouse. She doesn't mean to eavesdrop to the one-sided conversation he's having.

"I wish the Goddess I'd never laid eyes on you, Mimi."

There's silence while Mimi no doubt fills him in on what she thinks about their marriage too.

"Is there nothing you won't do for power? How many more members of our community have to disappear before you're satisfied?"

Frankie doesn't stay to listen to the rest of the conversation, instead transporting herself back to the main dock and making as much noise as she can on her return.

"Anyone home?" Even to her ears, her query sounds fake. Here's hoping Stanley buys it.

"I'll be with you shortly." Stanley's response confirms for Frankie he's still on the phone with Mimi. Not that she's going to move. She's staying exactly where she is.

"This is not over. I'll deal with you soon."

Of some surprise is that Frankie then hears what sounds like an old-fashioned receiver being slammed into its cradle. Who even has a landline these days?

"Come on down, Frankie."

While climbing down the ladder, Frankie's thoughts are in free fall. Does she question him about the *Syphonia*? Or does she admit she's overheard his conversation with Mimi?

Frankie starts out by acting as though nothing has happened. Unfortunately, she can't let it lie.

"Why didn't you say you knew how to get in touch with Mimi?"

"Ah, I thought I could sense someone up there."

It eventually comes out that in his position as coven leader his responsibility is to keep coven members safe. By telling Frankie how his ex-wife can be found he'd be putting her life in danger. "You've already shown yourself to be abysmal at following direct orders. At the very least you could find yourself locked up in *All Hallows Keep* and your powers, such as they are, taken from you."

"You didn't take my powers away because I visited the island, did you?" Sheesh, what is it with people stripping her of her powers in order to protect her? So far as Frankie can see, all this does is leave her vulnerable. She hates feeling this way. However, she's currently so angry she almost doesn't need any powers.

Stanley neither confirms nor denies why he's removed her powers. Instead he waves his hand absently over the surface of the coffee table, and a teapot, cups and saucers arrive on a tray. Frankie can see by the steam coming out of the spout that a brew is already underway.

"And the reason for your visit?"

Frankie fumes, fighting to get her anger under control. It's not lost on her that these anger issues have arisen since she received her new powers. But being manipulated as she is, she's got good reason to be irate. However her having a tantrum isn't going to do anyone any good, especially not her.

Stanley turns the teapot three times before pouring her a cup of what smells like jasmine tea. He then pours one for himself.

Frankie picks up her cup and takes a large gulp of too-hot tea and swallows it along with her irritation. Nope, it's not good enough. She takes another mouthful and repeats the process. Only then is she free to speak in a controlled manner. "I read something interesting in those photos of the pages about *All Hallows Keep*."

"Go on."

"There's mention of something called the *Syphonia*. From the way it was worded it sounds like this is how they remove powers from the inmates. This got me thinking, if they can take the powers away, surely they can put them back."

"They can. This happens when prisoners are released. Of course, in some cases their powers are reduced to avoid any re-offending."

"What if the powers were given to someone other than the original owner?"

Stanley dropping his cup of tea back on the saucer with a clatter tells Frankie he's come to the same conclusion as she has.

The one thing Frankie still hasn't worked out is why the Garnets, or the Werealls, would hand this sort of control over to someone like Stanley's ex-wife. It's something she muses out loud.

It turns out Mimi Merriweather is as addictive as crack cocaine and even deadlier. "Any man she latches onto doesn't stand a chance." Stanley's shudder is strong enough that his whole body gets in on the act.

"What does she look like?" Frankie tries to picture an old-aged femme fatale, failing miserably. Support hose are hardly likely to have a man losing his mind.

Stanley retrieves his wallet from the back pocket of his pants. Tucked in amongst a slew of receipts and small notes is a battered snap shot that he pulls free. He hands this over to Frankie as though it's precious. Frankie checks out the photo of a spritely older lady. Yes she's wearing a twinset and pearls; however it's a very stylish twinset and pearls. Even her tweed skirt is surprisingly fashionable.

While able to see how the woman in the photo would appeal to Stanley, Frankie has trouble seeing the woman as being addictive. At least not addictive enough that you'd put her in charge of somewhere like *All Hallows Keep*.

"Ah, Stanley?"

"Yes?"

"Why is Zane so dark on Mimi?"

Stanley doesn't answer to the point Frankie thinks he hasn't heard her. She's about to repeat her question when he speaks.

"I, ah, believe he was seeing her in the late 1800s."

Some quick mental calculations and Frankie comes to the conclusion that Mimi has to be pushing at least one hundred and forty. "I thought you said she wasn't a witch?"

"She isn't."

Frankie waits in vain for him to explain further. "Well if she's not a witch, what is she?" Even new to the magical world, Frankie knows any woman who's been around this long isn't a *Normal*. As to what she is that is the question. Here's hoping Stanley will tell her as she hates being kept in the dark.

"Mimi is a succubus." Stanley indulges in another shudder.

Okay, Frankie's heard the term. As to what it means, without Google, she's at a loss. Again, Stanley goes quiet on her. The pained look on his face points to him reminiscing about old times. It must have been quite the marriage to get this sort of reaction out of the coven leader.

"What is that exactly?"

Stanley looks up, taking his time to focus on her. "Oh. A succubus is a she-devil. They start by visiting you in your dreams, working their way into your subconscious like a maggot. When you meet them in person, it's already too late. You'll do anything to keep them happy, even hand over your soul."

This doesn't shine enough light on the subject to satisfy Frankie. Stanley once again loses himself in memories, and Frankie doesn't think she's going to get any more sense from him. She's pulled her phone out of her pocket and has started to search for more information, when he continues.

"As a powerful warlock, I should have known what she was and stayed clear of her. But, with her coming to me night after night in my dreams, I wasn't able to fight her off when she turned up in person. It was already too late."

Rather than suck the life and soul out of him and move on, Mimi had stayed with him long enough to give birth to Gwen, moving on soon after Gwen's second birthday.

"But you can relax. I don't think Zane is the focus of her attention, these days."

"These days? I should hope not." Frankie's mind goes into overdrive at thoughts of Zane locking lips with the old girl in the photo Stanley is gently sliding back into his wallet.

On noticing the care he takes with the snap shot, Frankie can see he's still not free of the woman's allure, even if thoughts of her revolt him.

"Mimi hasn't always looked like this. This photo has aged as she would have if we'd stayed together. She's able to take on whatever form is most pleasing to the man she's focusing on."

This throws a spanner in the works for Frankie. She's got no clue as to Mimi's appearance when she goes hunting for her. If she's with George Garnet she could either look like a woman suited to his age, or a twenty-something rich man's trophy girlfriend. And if the woman's got her claws into the Commander of the Werealls, will Frankie be faced with something resembling an explosion in a petting zoo?

6

Stanley is so lost in his thoughts that Frankie lets herself out and walks back down the pier to the *Pearl*. What if Mimi does go after Zane again? The woman being able to visit him in his dreams, means Frankie won't even be around to smack some sense into her.

And when was Zane going to mention he and Mimi had been an item back in the day? Never mind the day in question was long before Frankie was born. The angrier she gets about this, the more her powers surge. Her one hope is that it doesn't show because the last thing she needs is Stanley stripping her of any powers he missed earlier.

In combination with her anger at what feels

like Zane cheating on her is her worry he'll be okay going up against Calico Jack. It doesn't make sense that he's as determined as he is to get the printer and files back. Seems like overkill when he could so easily magic himself up a new printer, and maybe one with better functionality.

As to the files, she's already said she's got copies of everything. Maybe it's a guy thing? Perhaps he wants to prove a point? Or, maybe, just maybe, there's something he isn't telling her?

Her pent up energy stops Frankie from continuing to trawl through the screeds of information on *All Hallows Keep*. The emotions surging through her have her concentration shot to bits. "Come on Dex, I need to get this out of my system. Up you get."

He doesn't appear keen, and on closer inspection Frankie's able to see a slight blue tinge to the fur around his mouth. "What have you been up to?" She isn't concerned for his overall health, knowing his blue lips point to a surfeit of blueberries rather than a lack of oxygen. "Did you go over to Magda's while I was out?"

"I might have?"

"I'd say that's a yes. You're definitely coming for a run."

"I only had one."

"That's one too many. Up you get." At his continued lack of movement, Frankie points her finger at him and a moment later he's standing on the rug next to her.

She isn't sure who gets the biggest shock at this maneuver, her or Dex. She's never hit him with a spell like this before. He has to blink the sleep out of his eyes and it takes him a couple of wobbly steps before he gets his balance. Only on reaching the carpark is he firing on all cylinders.

Returning to the marina hours later, Frankie has her energy levels back under control, even if she's not as tired as she'd hoped to be. Dex on the other hand looks exhausted, with his tongue hanging out and his breathing heavy. He's also a lot slower than usual. On seeing the state of him, Frankie is overcome with remorse. She's never run him so ragged before. What is wrong with her?

"I think you deserve a muffin."

He perks up although not as much as usual.

"Make it two muffins, with cream. You've earned them." While he probably doesn't need them, her guilt sure as hex does.

His response is to follow her across the road

and into *Magic Beans*. He collapses on the floor next to her favorite table without as much as a peep.

Frankie is concentrating on breaking off small pieces of muffin and feeding them to the exhausted dog when she feels a presence. A small waft of aftershave confirms Zane is right behind her. On some level she already knew this. It's more a case of her ignoring his presence, like he'd ignored his dating history.

"Can I join you?"

Frankie shrugs before feeding another piece of muffin to Dex.

"What's wrong with Dex? He looks all done in."

Frankie keeps her back to Zane, not wanting to face him. "Our run was longer than expected."

Frankie continues to avoid looking at Zane, even when Mac, the café owner, puts a coffee down in front of him. It not being in a takeaway cup lets Frankie know she's going to have to face the Nautilus sooner or later. For one thing she's run out of muffins to feed to Dex. On the plus side, her familiar is looking a lot happier than he had been on their arrival at the café.

Frankie sits up straight and turns to face Zane. Perhaps it's her mutinous expression or her folding her arms tight that have him leaning away from her. Either way, he's looking cautious.

He goes from looking on edge to mystified before finally advancing onto understanding. "Ah, Stanley told you about Mimi."

Frankie responds with a curt nod. She knows if she opens her mouth, she's going to tell him what she thinks and it won't be pretty. Words like that are hard to take back.

"She appeared in half a dozen dreams and we went on a couple of dates. We weren't going steady, or anything." It turns out, once he realized Mimi was using him to get to his father, he dumped her. It wasn't something she'd taken well as he shouldn't have been able to do so once she had her claws into him.

It takes Zane saying over and over that he has no feelings toward Mimi other than loathing before Frankie relents. The huge slab of chocolate cake he buys her doesn't go astray either. Seriously, it's huge, with lashings of cream and toasted almonds. Hey, she's only human-ish. And the longer-than-usual run has left her hungry too.

Frankie's thinking about coming clean about her visit to the island when something occurs to her. Zane was already gone when she returned. And with him not knowing she's been, points to him having left without saying anything either.

While keeping quiet about her visit to the island appeals, it'll only be a matter of time before Stanley lets the Wereall out of the bag. Better she tells Zane when it's just the two of them.

His reaction is every bit as fiery as expected, with even Mac looking in their direction to see what's up. Rather than argue, Frankie deliberately goes on the defensive. Let's see him dig himself a nice deep hole that she can then metaphorically push him in.

Frankie pushes the remains of her cake around her plate, keeping her eyes downcast in the process. Avoiding eye contact will also make it easier to keep a straight face. "Zane, you were busy running the coven. I didn't want to bother you."

"More like you knew I'd try to stop you, so you avoided me."

Rather than acknowledge the truth of this, Frankie dips her finger in the remaining cream.

"Good Goddess, I wasn't in charge more than a matter of hours. How can you get into so much trouble in such a short time?"

Frankie doesn't answer him, using the excuse

of licking cream off her finger tip for her silence. Anyway, she doubts he's expecting one.

She waits until he runs out of steam before pushing her empty plate to the side. Oh, this is going to be so much fun.

"The fact you didn't know I was missing and the fact you were gone when I got back point to two things." Frankie holds her hand up so she can count them off. "Firstly, you didn't come looking for me to go with you when you took off after Calico Jack. Secondly, you had no intention of telling me you were going."

Zane squirms in his seat like a two-year-old and Frankie can't help but grin.

"I knew it would be dangerous, I didn't want you hurt."

Huh, two can play at that game. "Right back atcha, big boy."

"Big boy?" Now it's Zane's turn to grin.

"Yeah, well, you're taller than I am." Even though she's come up with this rejoinder, Frankie fails miserably at nonchalance with her face flooding with heat.

"So, did you find Calico Jack?" Frankie isn't expecting him to have done so, with the world a big place. Add to this her granddad being able to transport his launch the *Jolly Roger* to anywhere there's water, and the chances of discovery are slim at best.

Dex jumps up onto the spare chair at the table and looks first at Zane and then Frankie. *"Hah, and you say I can look smug."*

"You got that right, Dex."

For once her familiar only being able to communicate with her is a plus. He'd lost the ability after being Tasered at *Garnet Cove* and she'd thought at the time it would be a drawback. *"His supercilious smile says he found my disreputable granddad."*

"Where was he?"

"Still in the Caribbean as it happens."

"But how did you find him? He could have been anywhere."

"Frankie, if he's in salt water, he can't hide from a Nautilus."

Weird, if Frankie puts a seashell to her ear, all she can hear is the ocean. Looks like Zane has a better connection than she does.

"And?" Frankie winds her hand around in the air, letting Zane know she wants the story and she wants it in full with none of his usual editing.

While not recounting everything in fine detail, Zane doesn't leave anything out either. To be honest, Frankie's just as happy with the Cliff notes, with these being easier to remember.

"So he stole your laptop too? You never said that at Stanley's place."

"I didn't realize it at the time. It was a back-up laptop that I use for my work with the Nautilus Foundation."

"The Nautilus Foundation?"

"We, ah. We teach under-privileged kids how to swim."

Frankie is unable to stop a broad smile at thoughts of mer people teaching *Normals* how to swim. Those kids would freak if they knew the truth, with mermaids being right up there with unicorns when it came to childhood ideals.

"Wait, are unicorns real?"

"What?" Her sudden change of subject has obviously thrown him.

"Unicorns. Are they for real?"

"Of course not."

"Says the only guy at the table with a tail."

Dex coughs telepathically to get her attention. *"Puppy dog tails don't count."*

"But, you got your laptop back, right?"

Now it's Zane's turn to smile broadly. "Funnier to wait until they're ashore, sneak on board, copy all my files and then plant a virus. It's one not even those pirates will see coming."

"A computer virus?"

"Not exactly."

Despite her pressing him for more details, Zane won't budge. He instead turns the conversation back to her. "So what did you find on the island?"

Frankie skips through her trip to the island, right up to the point she saw the Wereall walking through the crack in the rock face.

"Werealls are dangerous creatures. How come you're back here and not missing, or dead?"

"I'm not stupid. I hit it with a freezing spell."

"Yeah, she's not stupid you know."

"No point, buddy. He can't hear you."

Zane, who's just taken a mouthful of his fresh coffee, spits it back out, narrowly missing Dex.

"That's not right. Magic doesn't work with Werealls."

"It worked alright. Not as well as usual, but it still held."

"So you actually froze a Wereall?" Without waiting for her response, Zane continues. "What did you do with it then?"

"Sent it back through the crevasse, closed the rock face back up and got the heck out of there."

Frankie's unable to stop herself from dusting her hands together in recognition of a job well done.

Zane speaks as though on auto pilot. "You sent it back through the rock face, closed it up and came home?"

On spotting the look of incredulity plastered on his gorgeous face, Frankie gets the impression none of this should have been possible.

Is it because she used her borrowed powers rather her witchy ones?

"I take it Stanley knows about this?"

Frankie leans on the table, her chin cupped in her hands. "Unfortunately, yes."

Zane looks at her, waving his hand in her direction. "He's taken your powers, hasn't he?"

Frankie doesn't have the luxury of time to mull this over. Does she tell Zane about the powers Stanley missed, or does she act as though she's once again powerless?

7

Frankie decides lying by omission is her safest bet. Frankie turns her back on Zane and shoves her hand down the neck of her t-shirt and retrieves the small folded map. All going well, this will work as the best distraction ever.

Zane's examination of the map is fleeting before he turns his gaze on her. Frankie's momentarily taken aback. Perhaps it's the light. She looks a little closer. Nope, she's not imagining things. His eyes are a deep green rather than their usual blue. She's wondering what this means when he interrupts her thoughts.

"Have you shown this to Stanley?"

"Not yet."

Zane stands abruptly, sending his chair flying.

Without letting go of the map, he makes contact with both Dex and Frankie, and transports all three of them to the main cabin on the *Annie*. Stanley looks to be as surprised by their arrival as Dex and Frankie are at having made the trip.

Dex who's landed on the sofa and rolled a couple of times, is hard up against Jojo. He narrows his eyes in Zane's direction. *"A little warning would be good."* He's not happy about the close quarters with Gwen's familiar, not that the Siamese looks chuffed about it, either.

Jojo places a paw on the small dog's rump, her claws popping out in a lethal Mexican wave. *"Get away from me flea-bag."*

"Huh, that's rich coming from the feline equivalent of a flea breeding facility."

Before an actual fight can start between the two familiars, Frankie scoops Dex up and puts him on the floor. She'd send him back to the *Pearl* but to do so would be to reveal her powers to Stanley and Zane.

"Dex is right, a little warning next time. Asking permission wouldn't go astray either." Frankie dusts herself off even though the move has been instantaneous. Her request falls on deaf ears with both Zane and Stanley bent over the map, their concentration absolute.

Only after ten minutes of this examination, does Zane lift his head. "Where did you get this from?"

In the knowledge she isn't going to be leaving any time soon, Frankie scoots a disgruntled Jojo to one side so she can sit down. Neither man speaks while she explains how it was she discovered the various layers of the map. On hearing she's used the services of a *Normal* Stanley looks to be as irate as he can be. Hmmmph, last time she checked nobody in the Marina Coven owned a printer set up the likes of Bruce's.

Frankie relaxes back into the sofa, safe in the knowledge that Stanley already thinks he's taken her powers away from her. This threat out of the way, there isn't much he can do. It's then she hears rustling from behind her. A quick peek over her shoulder shows Gwen the lizard to be sunning herself under one of the heat lamps, all while giving Frankie the evil eye.

Frankie is responsible for the coven leader's daughter being a lizard and locked up, meaning the animosity being directed at her is expected. What isn't expected is there are two slabs of marble, effectively dividing the glass case into three. That the space in the middle is worryingly empty isn't lost on Frankie.

Frankie doesn't think, she simply acts. If the coven leader thinks he's turning her into a lizard and locking her up between Gwen and George, he's in for a big surprise. Frankie touches the composite map with one hand and Dex with the other. She hasn't even had time to breathe before she, Dex and the map are in front of the familiar rock face.

If Stanley thinks he's going to turn her into a lizard to stop her from tracking down her dad, he's dead wrong.

A quick wave of her hand and once again Frankie and Dex are in their obnoxious tourist disguises. But, what if they run into the Wereall they'd seen earlier when dressed like this? Better if they're different altogether. "Hey Dex, what's your preference, Rottweiler or Alsatian?"

"Oooh, Rottweiler, please."

"Good choice."

Even Frankie will feel safer with a great hulking guard dog beside her. Thinking about her own appearance, Frankie channels her late mom and is soon the spitting image of the woman. Frankie pats her brunette bob into place, hitches up her mom jeans, and approaches the solid rock face.

As before her amulet lights up and the small

crack in the rock widens enough to allow her and Dex to venture forth. As when they'd seen the Wereall walking toward them, there's light streaming out of the gap. Not that this should be possible with the location of the crack in the rock. If anything they should be entering the depths of the island.

They're not half way through the gap when the rock starts to close behind them. This sees them explode out into the light on the other side just before the wall seals behind them. Two things are apparent. The light isn't from outside but rather a bright overhead lamp that illuminates the cave floor.

Frankie spins to face the wall of the cave where they've just entered. Rather than find runes as she's expected, she's faced with a surface that's free of any markings. She's close to discovering latent claustrophobia when she sees Dex is sniffing some markings further down the wall. And luck and these will allow her and her familiar to leave the cave the same way as they've entered.

Not that this is the only exit with the cave running in a straight line to the outside world. That there's an icy blast coming from this direction, means it's not an exit Frankie's keen on using. The temperature on the island on entering the cave had been hovering in the nineties, so wherever the cave leads to, it sure isn't *Garnet Cove.*

A quick check in the other direction shows a black so deep Frankie can't open her eyes wide enough to see anything. She's down on her hands and knees seeing if her amulet will re-open the chink in the rock when she hears voices.

"Dex, we need to hide."

Instead of responding, he looks at her, his head twisted to the side. While this looks cute on a Jack Russell, on a Rottweiler it's just plain weird. Blast, he isn't able to hear her. Pulling on some rusty charade skills, Frankie mimes that they need to hide. And fast. Frankie sees a space at the edge of the halo of light that's free of obstacles. It's small, but it'll do. She touches the top of Dex's head and transports them well away from the approaching pair.

Except that nothing happens. It looks as though it isn't just their ability to communicate telepathically that is on the fritz on this side of the rock face. Rather than allow him to walk freely, Frankie clambers to her feet and mimes patting her thighs. Dex jumps up, nearly sending her flying in the process. He's heavier as a Rottweiler. A LOT heavier. She staggers as quietly as she can, backing into the dark of the cave away from the voices.

That it's a male and female is evident by their voices. Also obvious is that the male sounds to have the head cold from Hades if you can even catch one somewhere that hot. As to what powers they have at their disposal, she's in the dark in more ways than one. Rather than walk quickly, Frankie slides her feet along the cave floor. This allows her to avoid the numerous rocks that would have her flat on her face if she tried moving any faster.

One thing that's moving at a rate of knots is her heart, with it hammering away in her chest. While Dex might be a ferocious guard dog on the outside, he's pure Jack Russell at heart. It's this that has him trembling like a jelly on top of a washing machine during the spin cycle. She isn't feeling too confident herself, not knowing if she's backing away from danger or into it.

There's a flash of light from the direction of the voices. It's enough for Frankie to see a large outcrop of rock and what looks like a side-tunnel. Frankie decides she's got a fifty-fifty chance of the approaching pair going that way, darting into the gap before they spot her.

This isn't easy when you're lugging a dog the

wrong side of one hundred pounds. Now her biggest hurdle is squeezing the pair of them as far back as possible and not grunting due to the effort required.

Dex safely down on the cave floor, Frankie gets down on her hands and knees next to him. Thank the Goddess she's wearing darker colors. Even Dex the Rottweiler is better suited to subterfuge than he would be with his standard Jack Russell coloring.

Another flare of light has Frankie moving into a crouching position. If she has to resort to martial arts to avoid her and Dex being captured, she needs to be ready. That's if her fighting skills work better in the cave than her magic does.

Frankie's body floods with adrenalin when lights in the cave flare even closer telling her the pair approaches. Here goes nothing.

She's ready to rush them, but they walk on by, apparently unaware of her and Dex.

While Frankie has been expecting a pair of Werealls, she's only right on one count. The male is Wereall right down to his mismatched head, torso, arms and legs. The woman, however, appears human, looks to be in her thirties and would be a shoo-in to win a beauty pageant. If it wasn't for the New York accent, Frankie could even mistake her for Magda in the half-light.

The light then goes out and another further along the cave flares into life. If Frankie hadn't just walked the same route as them, she'd think there were sensor lights at play. Is it that they've got some sort of device? Either way, Frankie wastes no time hefting Dex into her arms and inching her way back toward the light that pinpoints the exit. She simply wanted to check inside, not be stuck here for life.

Again, she slides her feet across the floor of the cave like an ice-skater and stubbing her toes a couple of times in the process. This has her making a note to herself to wear boots next time she comes back here. She knows she's definitely going to return as her gut is telling her the cave will lead to her dad. Not that she'll return on her own. While she has no trouble taking risks, she isn't stupid.

Frankie puts Dex down next to the rune markings on the wall where they'd entered. Thank the Goddess this spot is marked by the overhead light, otherwise she'd be stuck. A quick peek over her shoulder to check they're alone and Frankie gets close enough to the runes with her amulet that it lights up. The noise of the rock face opening is deafening and sure to be heard by the couple who'd passed earlier.

Frankie even sees the flare of light down the cave in that direction before the rock is open enough for her and Dex to squeeze through the gap. They don't dawdle this time. Both of them run full-tilt, exiting into the muggy heat of *Garnet Cove* in an ungainly tumble. Frankie scrambles to her feet and runs back to the cliff, putting her face right next to the runes. Her hope is that her amulet will stop the opening process. Nothing happens. The rock has stopped moving, in either direction.

"We've got company!"

Dex follows this up with uncharacteristic snarling that has the hairs on the back of Frankie's neck standing at attention. Then she realizes it's not Dex who's growling.

Jumping back, Frankie hits the Wereall and the woman with an immobilis spell. As before neither of them looks to be totally under the spell. Not wanting to risk her magic failing, she rockets them back through the crevasse fast enough that they slam into the wall on the other side of the cave. While they're still stunned, Frankie slams the rock face closed using her amulet. Not that she's going to trust the slabs of rock to stay this way.

They won't have long before the man and woman recover. She and Dex need to get out of here and pronto. It's where to go that's the dilemma. She doesn't want to go home in case they follow; she doesn't want to go to Zane's in case he gets hurt. If she goes to Stanley's place, she'll be sitting in that terrarium before you can say high-end handbag.

She's no closer to a decision when the break in the cliff face slams open with enough force that she and Dex are showered with hunks of rock.

8

Frankie arrives in the cabin of the *Annie* with Dex beside her. She's surprised to find Zane still standing next the coven leader. It must be serious for the Nautilus to be here an hour or so after she's left. So much for keeping him safe from the Wereall. Both men stare at her and Dex in astonishment.

Frankie jerks her head toward the terrarium. "Before you lock me in that thing, you might need my help." To make doubly sure she's safe from incarceration, she throws up a ward in front of herself and Dex without thinking too hard about it. Turns out she should have concentrated a little more.

Rather than magic filling the air between her

and the two men, there floats a solid sheet of purest crystal. Here's hoping it's strong enough to stop Stanley's skinx spell in its tracks. There's no way Frankie wants to spend the rest of her days as a glorified handbag under a heat lamp.

Stanley's mouth opens and closes a couple of times before he speaks. "Ah, I'm sorry, who are you?"

While Zane hasn't spoken, his stance tells Frankie he's ready to go on the attack. Good, because he might need to.

Frankie holds her arms out to the side to display the obvious. "It's me."

Dex barks telepathically to get her attention. *"Um, we're still in disguise."*

"Oh, sorry." Frankie waves her hands around herself and Dex and a moment later they're back looking like themselves.

"Awww, couldn't you have left me like that?"

While Frankie is comfortable to be back in jeans not quite so high-waisted, Dex is disappointed at no longer being in charge of so much *grrrr*.

Rather than their transformation eliciting a positive response from the two men, they drop into their respective seats, mouths agape.

Still not trusting Stanley to imprison her,

Frankie pulls out her wand. It's something that sees wands in the hands of the two men. *Bespelled bunnies.* This is not how she wanted things to go. The last thing she needs is to be crossing wands with these two.

Stanley staggers back to his feet, leaning heavily on the side of his chair to do so. "But your powers? I took your powers."

Zane drops his wand hand to his side and turns to Stanley. "I asked her if you took her powers. But..." Zane spears Frankie with a gaze before continuing, "She changed the subject. Do you think taking her powers was a good idea, considering?"

Frankie's gaze flits between the two of them. "Considering what?" Is there something they're not telling her?

Zane looks at her as if she's slipped a cog. "Ah, the Garnet family gunning for you, is as good a place to start as any. Then there are your relatives."

Unsure what Zane is on about with her relatives, Frankie looks at Stanley, "Yeah. What he says."

"I was hoping to stop you from returning to the island. At least in the terrarium, I know you'll be safe."

We'll that's just tough bucko. "If there's a chance I

can find my dad, nothing's gonna stop me. There also isn't a snowball's chance in Hades I'm subsisting on crickets and roaches."

Zane looks to be as annoyed as Frankie is feeling. "The island? Is that where you've been? After what I said?"

"Yes, yes. But never mind that. If they can follow me home, we're due company."

Zane launches himself to his feet, stalks over and stands unsettlingly close to the sheet of crystal. The merest tap with his wand and it shatters into a million pieces that then disappear. He's near enough she has to crane her neck to see his face. "How can disappear for all of a second, replace yourself and your dog, and get into so much trouble in such a short space of time?"

"What do you mean all of a second? I've been gone an hour at least."

"An hour?" Stanley sits back down again. "You entered the cave, didn't you?"

Frankie doesn't bother denying it, instead she rattles through events until she and Dex made it back to the island through the crevasse in the rock.

She's about to go on, but Stanley holds his hand up. "That your powers didn't work in the cave shouldn't have come as a surprise. You should remember that from what you read in *The Lore of*

Crafte. Of more interest is that the magic you performed before traversing the crevasse, stayed in place."

Frankie's immediately aware of the possibility this loophole would afford any raiding party. "That's true. This means I can conceal myself before I return."

"You're missing the point. Or should I say points? I took your magical powers away. Also no other magical entity traversing the crevasse has ever been able to maintain a spell after crossing over."

Zane nods in agreement. "It's the reason prisoners with magical powers can go in but can't get out. Even if they've got wards in place these fail as soon as they enter the cave. It's this that allows the Werealls to subdue them and strip them of their powers."

"Oh." Frankie makes a note to herself to conceal and protect her and Dex up the wazoo before she opens the rock face up again.

Zane stops the pacing that had been starting to get on Frankie's nerves. "Oh. That's all you have to say?"

Frankie hasn't cobbled together a better response when Stanley interrupts. "What happened after you crossed back to the island?"

"I'd activated the runes with my amulet and the rock face was closing, then it stalled. That's when the Wereall and the woman came through."

"The woman?" say Stanley and Zane in unison, with both their voices pitched higher than usual.

Despite Frankie describing her in as much detail as her memory will allow neither man shows any signs of recognition. This doesn't altogether surprise Frankie with both of them saying Mimi is able to take on the form most pleasing to whoever her latest target is.

"Hang on. If she's all decked out like a pageant queen, then surely her target isn't one of the Werealls. They'd be more attracted to something, well fluffier, wouldn't they?"

Zane is the first to start laughing. He's soon joined by Stanley.

How's she supposed to know Werealls can take on human form? Until a couple of days back Frankie thought *weres* of any kind were only found in romances. It sure as bent brooms hadn't been mentioned in Stanley's *Lore of Crafte*. Even back aboard the *Pearl*, Frankie's cheeks burn in remembrance of their laughter.

She also realizes she's gotten away from Stanley without being locked up and without him grilling her on the powers he hasn't been able to remove. It's a pity she forgot the composite map in her rush to get away.

"Dex, do you want to stay here while I go pick up another printout of the map?"

Because of the extra powerful wards Zane and Stanley have in place around the marina, Frankie knows he'll be safe from attack by a Wereall, or worse, Mimi. She also knows she's risking it by going to the computer shop. But she really does need to study that map and she'll be darned if she's going back to the *Annie* to be laughed at some more. Not that she's simply going to waltz over to *Bruce's Bits & Bytes* as bold as brass. Even she's not that brazen.

The first thing she notices on arrival is the over-powering aroma of coffee and muffins. It's the first time she's ever transported herself directly to *Magic Beans* and so is startled at how overwhelmed her senses are. The other unusual thing is that Mac is sitting on the barstool behind the counter rather than busy getting her order ready. That she's caught him unawares is obvious.

"Can I have two coffees and two muffins to go, please, Mac?"

"Ah, sure. I haven't had anyone sneak up on me like that in decades."

"Really? Not sure how I did that." This is a lie although only a little one. Her having transported herself here using her borrowed powers, there's nothing witchy for him to track. Still, the less he knows about her non-witchy powers, the better.

The paper bag of muffins stuffed in the front pocket of her hoodie, Frankie's able to hold a take-away cup of coffee in each hand. A quick scan out the door of the cafe shows the sidewalk to be empty, at least between here and *Bruce's Bits & Bytes*.

Head down, Frankie speed walks in the direction of the front door of the computer shop. She's close to running when she slams into someone right outside the shop. She's hit whoever it is hard enough that she comes close to dropping the coffees. On looking down at the pocket of her hoodie, her suspicion that the muffins have been squished completely is confirmed.

Frankie steps back to put some distance between her and the man she's run into. She isn't getting any bad vibes off him and so isn't too concerned. "I'm so sorry. I wasn't looking where I was going. Are you okay?" It's after she's asked this that she looks up. Then she's glad she's already spoken because words would fail her now. The guy is gorgeous. Heck, he even makes Zane look a little on the 'smacked by the ugly stick' side of things.

The blond god pushes open the shop door and steps inside, even holding it while she enters too. He then closes the door, and stays where he is, not going any further into the shop. It's after he smiles that Frankie realizes she's still staring at him. It's not her fault his dark brown eyes are almost hypnotic in their intensity. Frankie snaps her mouth shut, spins on her heel and flees toward the back of the shop. Only once she's safely past Mt Hard Drive does Frankie remember to breathe again.

Her plan had been to have a catch up with Bruce and use his crazy large screen to have a better look at the topography of the island. There's no way she's staying here now. It would be far too embarrassing. Luckily, the printout is ready and waiting for her, allowing her to hand the coffee over and drag the muffins out of her pocket.

"Sorry, they got squashed. They should be okay."

"I can cope with squashed if it's washed down

with one of your amazing coffees."

In return, he hands her a printout already rolled up and secured with a rubber band. "I, I can't stop today, things to do. And you've got a customer too."

"I do? That's weird. The buzzer didn't go twice."

Buzzer? What buzzer? It must be silent because she's never heard one on entering the shop. "He came in at the same time as me. Maybe that's it?"

Bruce puts his coffee and the paper bag down on the desk, before swinging around in his chair and lurching to his feet. He accompanies Frankie out to the front of the shop. Only there isn't anyone there.

"That's odd. He was standing right there." Frankie swings the rolled-up map wide and comes close to dropping her coffee again when she encounters something. It's something that isn't there on the face of things, not that she lets on. She even resists the temptation to shove the map under her arm so she can see if the cutie feels as good as he looks.

Instead she slides the map carefully into the pocket of her hoodie. Frankie then opens the door just wide enough to squeeze through before slamming it shut behind her. The merest glance through the glass front door shows her she's surprised Bruce with her weird behavior. Not that she can stay and explain. She hightails it for *Magic Beans* and immediately after walking through the door, transports herself back to the *Pearl*.

There is no way that guy was a warlock. While she hadn't been able to sense magic when her powers were fully under the jinx, she can now. And the more she gets them back, the better she's able to sense the paranormal. Even what she's thinking of as her borrowed powers allow her to do this. And she sure as Hades couldn't sense anything. It was like he was there, but he wasn't.

Dex, who's sitting on the window seat with his head hanging out one of the windows at the back of the vessel, swings in her direction. He looks first at her coffee, then the rolled-up map that's poking out the pocket of her hoodie. *"Where's my muffin?"*

"Sorry, I ran into someone and it got squished." Even thinking about the guy has Frankie licking her lips. After putting the map and her coffee down on the sideboard, she transports herself back to *Magic Beans*, again taking Mac by surprise.

But he's not alone in being surprised. Sitting at her table and looking like he owns the place is the blond god. That he's eating what looks to be the last blueberry muffin has Frankie glaring at him. It's something he appears surprised by. Perhaps he's used to women fawning over him rather than scowling?

He doesn't know what grief she's going to get if she has to go home to Dex without a muffin. If he wasn't in the process of licking all the frosting off the top of said muffin, she'd be tempted to grab it off him and scarper.

"Mac I don't suppose you've got any more blueberry muffins out back?"

Mac smiles broadly. "I think I can rustle something up."

It takes a second for Frankie to see the large plate in the glass case is groaning with a fresh supply of Dex's favorite treat.

Mac's bagged a couple for her and is handing them over, when she leans forward so she can speak to him as quietly as she can. "Mac, the blond guy in the corner, what is he?"

Mac keeps his voice just as low when he responds, "Him? He's a Wereall."

Frankie has a flash-back to walking in the front door after school with a mangy pup that had followed her home. She doubts Zane and Stanley would be as keen as her mom had been if she asks if she can keep this particular stray.

9

F rankie can't believe one of those things managed to track her down after all. She also can't believe that the pile of animal parts she observed in the cave can transform into such a cute human. Definitely not one as cute as that she saw at *Bruce's Bits & Bytes* and later at *Magic Beans*. That Mac had derision in his voice on confirming the blond Adonis as a Wereall hasn't been lost on Frankie.

Whether this is down to a history that's complicated or good old-fashioned jealousy she isn't sure. Either way, she isn't hanging around to find out. Any luck and the protections Zane and Stanley have placed on the marina will keep him at bay and not top-side on the *Pearl*.

Handing the muffins over to Dex, she once again transports herself down to the *Annie*. While Stanley is there, Zane is missing. Here's hoping he hasn't popped over to the café for a top-up of caffeine. Two guys like that in a space as small as *Magic Beans* could see fur and scales flying before you could shout alpha male.

The one negative in all of this is that Frankie hasn't seen any sign of the woman she suspects is Mimi. It would be so much easier to get hold of her if she simply rocked up. She wonders if Stanley's ex-wife is even aware the Wereall has tailed her back here.

Stanley looks up at her. There isn't a hint of surprise on his face this time. "I wondered when I'd see you again."

"We, ah, could have a problem."

"Yes, Mac tells me one of them managed to track you back here. No surprise really with their sense of smell being what it is."

Frankie bristles before he explains they can latch onto something as small as a single scent molecule rather than her being in need of a shower and some deodorant. "It might also be that the creature senses familiarity in you."

Now it's Frankie's turn to drop into one of the lounge chairs. "Familiarity?" Even though she's asked, she's got a good idea where things are heading. Or should that be *Were* things are heading? It's not a direction she's keen on, although it would explain why it is she's able to keep her magic after crossing the crevasse.

"But I've never managed to change myself into part anything."

"And yet you managed to transform yourself well enough that Zane, Magda and I were unable to recognise you, even using our magic." It turns out that a transformation by a witch or warlock is an illusion. It's one that can be sensed if you have enough power. Apparently when Frankie does it now, it's as though she truly is someone else. "When you first arrived here channeling an older lady, it was as though you were who you portrayed to be. You even sounded completely different."

Frankie slumps down even further in the chair. "This is so not good."

"It's not the end of the world. In fact it might even help you to free your father from *All Hallows Keep*."

"Does this mean I'm going back?"

"Not just you. Zane's already putting together a group who'll be suited to the sort of rescue mission you'll be on."

"Does this mean you're coming too?" Sure the

guy is powerful but images of what amounts to a senior's day out assail Frankie. It would be the odor of *Bengay* rather than her concealment spell failing that would give them away.

"Unfortunately not. Those who traverse the crevasse must have strength without the need to resort to their powers."

"So, that's Magda and Zane. Who else?"

"For something as important as this, we're recruiting outside of the coven, and even outside of our species."

And just like that, Frankie's imagination goes into overdrive, with her not even needing to close her eyes to see Ironman and Aqua Man as part of the group. Technically they've already got their own version of Aqua Man in the form of Zane. Frankie can't wait to see who their equivalent of Robert Downey Junior is going to be.

It's something that must show on her face, as the next thing she's aware of is Stanley clicking his fingers not an inch from her nose. "Good Goddess Frankie, concentrate."

She doesn't like being chastised for her lack of attention, not that she doesn't deserve it. What is wrong with her these days? She never used to have this much trouble staying on track.

Stanley casually puts a hand on her shoulder.

Before she has time to think, they're sitting at her favorite table at *Magic Beans*. Jinxed jellyfish she hasn't even had time to think about what her coffee order will be. Something that causes her even more consternation is the unwanted visitor is still sitting there although he's finished his coffee and muffin. That he deliberately looks at her while licking a hint of frosting off his top lip does funny things to her stomach. No doubt as intended.

"William, I wondered if it might be you." Despite the reservation in Stanley's voice, he still holds his hand out to shake with the Wereall, although it's a while before this happens. It's getting to the point of being insulting before their visitor takes up Stanley's offer and shakes. Even then Frankie is able to see he uses more force than is necessary with the ends of Stanley's fingers going white from lack of blood.

Good looking and a jerk, there's a combination she's seen before. He'd better behave himself or he'll find all his worldly goods stacked on a bonfire, same as happened to her ex when he crossed her.

With fire out of the question, Frankie wonders if it's good form to throw a glass of water over an alpha male trying for a show of supremacy. It works with dogs although she doubts it'd be appreciated in this instance.

As if things couldn't get worse, Zane then pops into view and takes the only spare seat at the table. Goodness, the last time Frankie saw this much testosterone in one place was at an MMA competition. Actually, stitch that. The MMA comp was tame compared to this.

It doesn't matter how many ways Zane and Stanley ask William, he keeps to his story of just being in the neighborhood. They all know it's a lame excuse, even him. Not that he can be persuaded to reveal his real reason. He also denies knowing anyone of Mimi's general description(s). Getting to his feet, he politely says goodbye and walks out the door. For Frankie it's a complete letdown with her expecting something far more spectacular than this. She would have liked to have seen even a hint of fur or a change of body parts instead of this pedestrian exit.

Zane and Stanley however breathe a combined sigh of relief. Even Mac looks happy to no longer be host to one of the Werealls. Only when sure their unwanted visitor isn't going to return and wreak havoc, does Zane look at Frankie. "You know who he was, don't you?"

I'm guessing he was the guard I sent back through the fracture in the rock.

"Hardly," snorts Stanley. We've just been given the rare privilege of a visit from William Were, the Sovereign Head of the Werealls.

"Oh, that's just peachy." This is definitely one of those times Frankie would rather life had thrown the garden variety whatever at her rather than the super-duper version of surprise. For the head honcho to be paying them a visit, she knows it's bad. But then, isn't it always?

Zane also looks to be experiencing disbelief. "I still can't believe he didn't try to take you with him."

Frankie sits up straight in her seat. "Take me with him? Why would he take me with him?"

Zane doesn't stop with one reason, instead counting out four that he can think of, off the top of his head. If you look at it that way, she guesses it does sound bad. Not that she's done anything on purpose, with every transgression being down to bad luck rather than good management. Surely that counts in her favor?

Rather than dwell on Frankie's litany of sins

against the Werealls, Stanley looks at Zane. "Did you manage to find the people you were after?"

"I did. And they didn't want a bar of it. I'm afraid to say there'll just be the four of us."

Frankie looks at Stanley, not that he returns her gaze. "I thought you said you wouldn't be going."

"I'm not. I think the fourth member of the group Zane is referring to is young Dex."

"I don't want him going back there. Even if I turn him into a Rottweiler again, without our ability to communicate, he'll be a hindrance rather than a help." Not that Frankie would voice this concern if her familiar was present. He likes to think he's tough, and she's happy to keep him under that illusion.

Stanley takes a sip of tea from the cup Mac has put in front of him before putting it carefully back in its saucer. "Your communication will only be affected while you're in the cave. Once you get out of the cavern and onto the barren island that's home to the *Keep* you'll be able to communicate as freely as you do here. At least this is what *The Lore of Crafte* says."

"So, we're leaving today?"

"Unfortunately, no," says Zane. "We need to teach Magda the basics of hand-to-hand combat in case she isn't able to draw energy once we're out of the caving system. History says I won't be able to use my powers there and so chances are she'll be the same."

"If I hit us with a concealment spell, she won't need to. So long as we're sneaky, we should be fine."

"And if that only works for you and Dex? It might be because the two of you are linked that he remained invisible? What happens to Magda and me if we cross the fissure to find ourselves as plain as day?"

He's got a good point. And while he's not exactly weak without his powers, Frankie isn't sure about Magda. She's got strength, but does she have technique?

"I'll go let her know training starts immediately." This is an assumption on Frankie's part. Although, knowing Zane like she does, she can guarantee this will be his plan. A curt nod confirms it.

Rather than go straight to *The Crate*, Frankie transports herself back to the *Pearl* to check on Dex. Not that this is all she's going to do. A quick sip of her coffee lets her know that it's cold enough to chug. And this is just what she does as she knows she'll need the caffeine if Zane trains like he always does.

"Wakey wakey sleepy pup." Frankie runs her hand down Dex's spine and he arches into her palm, even though he's not fully awake. "How would you like to learn some fighting techniques?"

His head pops immediately. *"Me? Can I do that?"* If anything, his reaction has been even stronger than her mentioning muffins.

"I don't see why not? Remember when we were at *Garnet Cove* and you helped me by tripping those guards?"

Frankie can see that although he's trying to remember, he's coming up empty. It might well be that any tripping on his part was unintentional with him even coming close to tripping her once or twice. "Come on, we need to go get Magda and then we're training at Zane's place."

It's after dark before Zane is happy with their progress, leaving Magda, Frankie and Dex unsteady on their feet. The first obstacle they'd encountered was Magda not being able to staunch her ability to drain their energy when she was under attack. No matter how hard she tried. This was solved by Frankie shielding herself and Dex with her new powers, and Zane doing likewise to himself using good old-fashioned witchcraft.

Before this there had been discussion about warding the energy vamp, lots of it. Then Magda herself had deemed it too dangerous without giving any reasons why.

The issues around energy having been solved, it had been all on, with Frankie and Zane first taking Magda through some rudimentary moves. Because of her strength and natural grace, she picked these up with ease. It was a different story with Dex whose ability to trip was perhaps too good. But, eventually the four of them settled on a technique of diversion, trip, thump and repeat. It was the repeat that's seen them wiped out on the energy side of things.

Zane sees Magda, Frankie and Dex to the door; seemingly back to his usual levels of energy. "Two more days of this and we'll be good to go."

"Two more days?" say Frankie and Magda in unison, with even Dex chiming in telepathically.

Magda puts her hand on Frankie's shoulder to stop herself from swaying. "Frankie, are you able to take me to a place where there are lots of people?"

"Would a sports bar do?"

Magda smiles broadly. "That would be perfect."

Even though Frankie's physical reserves have been tapped by the overly long training session, her magical powers are still strong. It takes seconds to have Dex back on the *Pearl* with his dinner organized. She then takes Magda out for a 'drink'. And while she could have transported them all over town, it's decided the Toyota will be better suited to their requirements in this instance.

After two sports bars, a restaurant and a passing motorcycle gang, both girls are glowing with good spirits. Magda's easily able to pull on the energy from the comfort of the car, drawing it to her and subsequently passing any spare onto Frankie. Rather than focus on any individual, Magda takes a little from each patron to avoid anyone keeling over.

That is until Frankie spots an unsavory individual harassing a girl outside a bar they're parked across from. All Frankie has to do is point the loathsome creature out to Magda and next thing the guy's flat on the ground. Much as Frankie wants to get out of the car and go over and put the boot in, her bed has more appeal. Frankie's edging the car out into traffic when she sees the girl they've saved up-end her drink over the guy on the ground. That a couple more girls join in confirms for Frankie and Magda that taking the guy out was the right choice. They're quiet on the drive home, with each of them deep in thought.

Frankie has even parked the car and is locking the car door before Magda speaks again. The energy vamp leans on the hood, and says, "We do this again before we return to the Cove, yes? It was fun, yes?"

"I'd be up for that. A quick side trip to Times Square or some seedy bar somewhere should see us all nicely topped up." Although thoughts of Dex with a surfeit of energy have Frankie dropping the keys before she can shove them in her handbag.

Something else that slows her is thoughts of seeing her dad within days.

What shape will he be in?

Will he be a jerk like Calico Jack?

How will he take the news his wife is dead? Knowing she'll be the one who has to break this news has her heart stuttering in her chest.

10

T hree full days pass before Frankie stands at the cliff face with the others. Three days of hard training followed by visits to various drinking establishments to top up their energy levels. While it had been just Magda and Frankie the first night, the other nights have seen Zane and Dex along for the bar crawl too. Sure, Zane is strong as an ox, he's also no-one's fool and so if there's energy going begging, he's not going to say no.

Of surprise to Frankie has been Zane not going all alpha male on them and insisting they take his car. It was then she discovered he doesn't even own a car. "Why bother when I can transport myself anywhere I want to go on land."

Frankie knows he doesn't have any trouble

travelling by water, with that tail of his able to move him around as speedily as if he's fitted with an outboard motor, albeit whisper-quiet.

Something else that's quiet is the surrounding jungle. She can't even hear one of those parrots that normally don't seem to be able to shut up. It's noticeably quieter than the last time she stood in front of the cliff. The other difference is that the heart with her grandparent's initials in it has a few extra embellishments.

These new additions, along with the sensation they're being watched has Frankie hitting the four of them with a spell of concealment. It's one that has them visible to each other, while safely hiding them from anyone else. That she's crossed her fingers while performing the spell is something Zane notices, not that he comments on it.

The hackles on her neck settle back down and she turns from her friends to the cliff. She's about to speak when something occurs to her. No point being invisible if you're then going to yabber out loud. Another casual wave of her hand and she knows their words will remain between themselves.

This isn't all that occurs to her. If the Werealls' sense of smell is as good as Stanley says it is, them being invisible and quiet will be pointless. She has to think about it for a second before she comes up with something she hopes might work. They'll know soon enough.

Frankie looks for the runes on the cliff face. "That's weird."

Zane moves to stand next to her. "What is?"

"The runes I used to open the crevasse. I can't see them."

There's a small pause, before Frankie and Zane speak in concert. "William!"

Magda moves over to stand on Frankie's other side. "The way, it 'as been blocked?"

Zane smacks his hand against the cliff face in frustration. This is mild compared to what Frankie wants to do. They've come too far and worked too hard, to be stalled now. It's also about now Frankie wishes she'd taken the time to memorize the incantation from *The Lore of Crafte* that would see the rocks opening without her amulet interacting with the runes.

Not keen on missing out on anything, Dex pokes his head between Frankie's legs. *"What are we looking for?"*

"The runes, buddy. They're not here anymore."

Perhaps using the incantations it what allows Mimi to come and go as she pleases. From what Stanley has said of the woman, Frankie wouldn't put it past her to be checking out *The Lore of Crafte* while her husband was asleep.

Frankie is making a mental note to ask the coven leader about this when Dex sneaks between her legs. He then has a good scrabble amid the leaf litter that's piled up at the base of the cliff. Next thing Frankie knows, clods of dirt and pebbles are raining down on her feet as Dex does what terriers do best.

Maybe she should have turned him into an Alsatian as he'd begged for. At least those brutes didn't dig like this. She's about to tell him to knock it off, but he speaks inside her head stopping her admonishment where it is.

"Is this what you're looking for?"

Dropping to her hands and knees next to her familiar, Frankie's able to see what it is he's uncovered. On getting closer her amulet lights up as she's expected, and the rock splits in two. It's not as wide as the last time Frankie opened it, and while it'll be a tight squeeze, there's enough space for all of them to get through. Not that they waste time in the crevasse with Frankie knowing all too well how quickly it can close.

Sure enough, Frankie who's at the rear with Dex in her arms is soon hard up against Magda and Zane in an effort to have them moving faster.

The sensation of the two rock faces grinding together right behind her would be enough to make anyone hurry.

They burst into the cave with little regard for the amount of noise they're making. Thankfully, the space is as deserted as it had been last time Frankie and Dex arrived. They've been lucky. Very lucky.

Again, there's a chill wind blowing from the direction of the cave mouth and the direction they're going to be heading in. It's this that has all of them dressed in winter woolies, right down to thermal underwear. Even Dex is sporting a very smart quilted coat and little rubber booties.

They're moving toward the mouth of the cave, when Dex runs in front of them and, unable to communicate telepathically, points like a hunting dog in that direction. They're about to have company. The small dog then does an about-turn and starts to sniff his way along the ground. Knowing where it is he's off to, Frankie catches up and clips a lead onto his collar. She then motions for the others to get in behind and fast.

They're soon swallowed up by the intense black of the cave, with Magda holding onto the back of Frankie's jacket and Zane bringing up the rear. It's a tight fit in the side passage Frankie's hidden in earlier. Surely with their dark colored clothing, they should be good?

This time it's two guys who pass and who they get a good look at courtesy of the sensor lights going on. That the four of them haven't activated the sensor lights is both good and bad because it looks as if the guards are able to activate the lights as they pass, or perhaps even all at once. There'll be no hiding if this happens.

Only after they can no longer hear the two We-realls, do the four of them sneak out of their hiding place. They then retrace their steps, moving as fast as they're able to in the half light. Only when it's light enough, does Frankie unclip the lead from Dex's collar. Eventually they get to a point that their way is brightly lit by the light streaming in from outside although this slows them down in its own way. They have no idea what they're going to be facing on their arrival with *The Lore of Crafte* light on details about that.

Zane waves his hand to get everyone's attention, bringing them together in a huddle reminiscent of a college football game. "Do we remember the drill if we meet anyone from here on out?" Even though his words are whispered, they bounce around the cave, echoing backward and forward before dying away. No one moves, or even breathes; waiting to hear if this has given them away.

There being no reaction to Zane's words, they turn to face the mouth of the cave.

There'll be no hiding from here. The sides of the man-made, or at least Wereall-made, straight-away in front of them are glassy and smooth. They're halfway to the cave mouth when they hear voices. Without access to her powers Frankie has never felt so vulnerable in her life although based on experience this would be when they'd fail her, anyway. She hopes her concealment spell is still in place or they're going to be in for a heap of trouble.

Although with adrenalin surging through her body, it might even be better if they do have to fight their way out of the cave. The Goddess knows it can take ages for the buzz to fade of its own volition.

Frankie, Magda and Dex stand ready to go on one side of the cave, while Zane stands ready on the other. To the casual observer, the group looks to be relaxed. They're anything but. It's therefore a complete let down when two Wereall guards enter the cave from outside and start walking toward them. That the Werealls then march between them as though they're not there has Frankie punching the air in a silent yes! This means all three of her spells worked.

She steps in behind the pair, ready to take them out and has crept forward a single step when she sees Zane frantically waving out the corner of her eye. He draws his finger across his throat before putting it to his lips in a non-verbal 'Don't do anything and don't say anything'. It's either that or 'Take out the guards and keep quiet while you're at it'. Frankie is leaning toward the former, especially with there being nowhere to stow the guards. That is without traipsing all the way back to that side passage.

Even Dex has picked up that he's supposed to stay put although he leans out as the Werealls pass him and has a good sniff. It's something the guards must sense, with both of them spinning on the spot, obviously expecting to find someone behind them. Broken broomsticks, it looks as if the spell of silence has failed, she hopes the concealment and deodorant spells stay in place. Frankie freezes, taking the opportunity to examine the Wereall guards. Perhaps the creepiest thing about the conglomeration of animal parts standing in front of her is the very human eyes staring back.

"Breath of a dog, now I'm hearing things as

well as seeing them," says the one on the right. "That woman has us working far too hard."

"Yeah, pretty on the outside. Ugly as sin on the inside," says the other. "I dunno what the boss sees in her."

They swing on the spot and continue on their way, with the lights blinking on and off to match their pace. Only after there's no sign of the two guards or lights, do the four of them move quietly toward the cave mouth and the light streaming in.

Not that they march straight out into the open. Flattening themselves against one wall, they inch forward until Frankie is able to see what lies beyond. *Club Med* it most definitely is not.

Even the Mohave Desert is teeming with life compared to the barren outcrop of rock that looks to be the size of a city block. It's surrounded by sea and sky just as gray, adding to the depressing air. It's as though every bit of color has been wrung out of the place, on purpose. Never mind the prisoners, how on earth to do the guards put up with the conditions?

Atop this pile of misery is *All Hallows Keep* itself. Even having seen an illustration of the *Keep* in *The Lore of Crafte*, Frankie shudders at the real thing. Hewn out of the very granite it stands on, it's a gray building in a gray world. Frankie doesn't care what she has to do; she's not leaving this place without her dad. Any luck and he'll be nicer than Anne Bonny and Calico Jack, the two relatives she's met to date. It shouldn't be hard.

One thing in their favor is that the place looks to be deserted. Putting her head out of the cave as far as she dares, Frankie's unable to see any watch towers, or even any guards walking the no-man's-land that surrounds the *Keep*. Not that there would be anywhere to go if you did try to swim for it.

Frankie ducks back inside, beckoning everyone to move closer. "The way looks to be clear and there aren't any watch towers. I can't see any action at all."

Zane has a quick look himself before rejoining the group. "We'll have to move carefully. Just because you can't see them, doesn't mean they're not there. Werealls are masters of illusion allowing you to see what you want to see."

Frankie gulps at this snippet. Maybe William isn't as good looking as she thought. Maybe it was all her imagination? And if it was, what on earth was she doing imagining up someone the polar opposite of Zane?

There's no point in delaying the rescue mission any longer, and the four of them sneak out of the cave. Keeping close to the water-line to avoid running into any Wereall guards by accident, they work their way around the island to what looks to be the back of the *Keep*. There are so few windows and obvious entrances, it's hard to tell. Taking in the solid wall of granite in front of her, Frankie suspects this is going to be as good as it gets. The side they're looking up at is completely devoid of windows or doors, and Frankie can't decide if this is a good or a bad thing.

Scurrying across the rocks and expecting a cry of alarm any second, eventually they stand with their backs hard against the wall itself. The choppy sea watching them, Magda, Frankie and Zane rotate to examine the wall. This close up, the height of the wall is even more intimidating. No wonder there aren't any escapes on record. If the fall didn't finish you off, you'd drown trying to swim your way to freedom.

It's on looking back at the gray water in contemplation of the obstacles they're facing that Frankie sees the first telltale fin. What was she thinking; of course the sea surrounding the chunk of rock is teeming with sharks.

Beside her Frankie is conscious of Magda jumping up and down, getting progressively higher with each leap. Unfortunately she tops out at around twenty feet, falling short of reaching the top by around one hundred and sixty by Frankie's reckoning.

Frankie can think it's safe to say Magda has no access to her powers of transportation or energy vacuuming here. This has Frankie thumping the wall. "How on earth are we supposed to get inside, short of flying or dynamite?" Blast it, where is Sophie the witch with a knowledge of explosives when you need her?

Much as it would be a lot easier to simply walk through a door, the few they've spotted look to be made of solid iron. Frankie could achieve this with magic. Although once through, they might walk smack bang into a whole stack of Werealls.

It's much better to scale the walls and take their enemy by surprise or sneak in undetected, altogether.

They're still standing looking up at the *Keep* working on a plan to get inside when Frankie hears Dex humming inside her head. Funny, she hadn't even thought about trying to use her own magic since leaving the cave. This has her experimenting with transporting a small rock nearby and confirming her powers are back. As to their levels and stability that's anyone's guess.

Unsure if the Werealls not seeing them in the cave was a one-off, Frankie hits all of them with another concealment spell as well as the spells of silence and deodorant. And for once she feels as though they're going to stick, with her sensing her magic has a stability to it here that's sadly lacking in her own realm. Now all they need to do is get into what looks to be an impregnable fortress. Mind you, if it's been designed like most prisons, it'll be intended to keep people in, and not out.

Before Frankie knows what she's doing, she's a foot off the ground. It's nothing as clever as levitation, rather her having climbed there using rocks jutting out from the wall. Looking up, she can see enough protuberances to have the outside of the *Keep* resembling the beginners' wall at a climbing gym. This will make getting in a piece of cake.

It'll be getting back out that will prove challenging. Not able to sense the *American Pearl* after crossing the crevasse, Frankie's unable to retrieve any ropes they could use to abseil down the walls. Nope, they're going to have to leave through one of the few doors they've spotted. If needs must.

Frankie's made it three feet off the ground when Zane plucks her off the wall and puts her back down.

"Much as I admire your spunk, Shortcake, I don't think that's a good idea."

"It would get us to the top."

"It could also get us to the bottom faster than we'd like."

Broomsticks and botheration, he's got a point. But if they're not going to risk climbing how are they supposed to get over the top? It's then Frankie notices Magda looking at her in a manner that fills her with dread.

11

Frankie rubs her hands up and down her arms in an effort to quell her sense of unease. Not that it does any good. They can't give up and go home now. Not after coming so far.

Frankie's readying herself to fight to stay on alone if needs be, when Magda speaks.

"You 'ave made the little rock move. Yes?"

"Ah, yes."

Magda holds her arms wide. "Now you try with me."

Frankie balks. It's one thing to transport a rock from one spot to another without touching it. It's another to move a woman she counts as a friend. "What if I move you the wrong way and you end up in the sea? I'm not that sure of my powers here." Even if they're relatively stable, she doesn't exactly know what she's doing with them. Or is it that her magic has gone wrong so many times that she's lacking the nerve to try something new?

Zane moves to stand atop a rock that's the size of an apartment-sized fridge. "Why don't you practice with something bigger and work your way up from there?"

This she can do, waiting until Zane is back beside her before trying.

It's so easy that she has trouble believing she's the one who's done it. Only after she's moved half a dozen more rocks and boulders of progressively larger size, does she move Zane. Again, it's as easy as breathing. Next she tries moving Magda and Zane together, then them along with Dex.

There's still one small problem they haven't discussed. It's one that's been at the back of Frankie's mind. "I can't just transport us inside when we don't know what we'll be facing. What if I transport us into the middle of a cell, or worse, the shower block?"

Zane does the eyebrow raise thing that he seems to reserve for her.

Okay if he's doing that, then there's something she's missing, with it not coming to her until after her brain starts to smoke. She tries with a small pebble, then a rock and finally moves onto one of the fridge-sized boulders. This could work. This could work better than simply moving all of them from one spot to another. At the very least they'll be able to check the place out on the sly rather than simply arriving the Goddess knows where.

The question is can Frankie levitate herself at the same time as the others?

She soon has herself floating a foot above the ground. She then concentrates on the others and soon they float up to join her, with them hanging in the air like a still life. Frankie can't stop her huge grin at this achievement. This falters when she thinks about them all hovering several hundred feet in the air. It's enough to have them earthbound soon after.

Can she trust herself with the lives of the other three? While Zane and Magda look ready to go, Dex appears nervous. Might it be he's picked up on her jitters like he has in the past? Then she thinks of her dad stuck in this place and all doubts flee.

She can do this.

She has to.

Frankie looks around the group, taking special notice of Dex. "Are we all ready?" All three of them nod although Dex's nod is less emphatic than those given by Zane and Magda.

A deep breath and Frankie has the four of them suspended a couple of inches off the ground. Frankie then clips the lead back onto Dex's collar and winds the end around her wrist, holding it tightly. Even if they do have a special bond, she knows she'll be happier with them leashed together. On seeing her small pal relaxing, she knows he's the same.

Slowly they start to rise next to the wall. They then speed up a little as Frankie gains in confidence. Then they're rising faster and faster and Frankie worries she's going to overshoot the top of the *Keep* walls by several hundred feet. Zane gritting out "concentrate" next to her, has her doing so and they slow back down.

Rather than float above the top of the walls where they might be seen, Frankie levitates them to where they're able to peek over the top of the parapet. What's in front of them isn't what any of them is expecting. Rather than be looking down into the *Keep*, they're faced with a solid granite roof. There isn't a skylight, chimney or structure in sight, just a huge expanse of gray rock.

Frankie floats them up and onto the roof, setting them down without as much as a bump. It's something she's very proud of and she knows she's done good work when Zane throws his arm around her shoulders and squeezes her tight.

While Frankie, Zane and Magda stand looking at the rock expanse in front of them, Dex's inquisitive nature has him walking forward sniffing. If Frankie didn't know better, she'd think he was on the trail of something and she unclips his leash and shoves it in the pocket of her puffer jacket. She's still wondering what Dex is on the trail of when he steps forward and disappears through the solid rock. It's quick thinking on her part that has him rising up again. If a dog could go white, Dex is giving it a pretty good go.

Only after she's cuddled him enough that he stops shaking, does she ask him what he's seen. Doggy gibberish is all he can come up with.

"Zane, hold my feet." Frankie lies full-length on the solid rock and inches her way forward until the rock disappears beneath her. Tilting forward from her waist, she dips down through the mirage of rock, closing her eyes against the solid wall of gray as it's creepy as heck.

Dropping forward as far as she can, she opens her eyes. Then she's spouting as much gibberish as Dex had, unable to comprehend what it is she's seeing. One thing that's definitely not good is one of the Wereall guards looking straight at her. She isn't sure if she's visible or causing a break in the mirage that is the roof of this building from hell.

Horrified by what she's seen, Frankie levitates herself free of the mirage. She'd glad Zane's holding her feet when she shoots up with enough force that she lifts him off the ground. Only Magda grabbing onto the pair of them keeps them from disappearing into the gray ceiling of cloud that fills the sky in all directions. This does however give Frankie an idea as to how to use her new skill as a means of attack.

It takes a lot of measured breathing on her part to get her heart rate back to normal, allowing her to speak. "I spotted a way in."

However brief her a glimpse of what lay below, it's been enough for Frankie to see there's a solid rock staircase on the other side of the *Keep*. All they need to do is crawl their way around there, keeping a hand over the edge of the hidden parapet until they touch the start of the stairs.

The edge of the gaping hole being hidden by the mirage, there's no way any of them want to walk around freely. The other unknown is if the guard is going to come to investigate the break in the mirage, or even Frankie herself, if he's seen her. However, his look of puzzlement rather than a cry of alarm points to her having remained invisible.

After crawling far enough, they find the top of the staircase. It's wide enough to allow all four of them to clamber down the first few steps lizard-like. This has their heads clearing the mirage but their bodies hidden. At least Frankie hopes their bodies are hidden. It could be that those inside are able to see out for all she knows.

All four of them clear the mirage at the same time, swiveling their heads in all directions to give the place the once over as quickly as possible. They allow themselves five seconds before retreating back to the relatively safety of the flat roof.

Frankie dusts the front of her jacket free of grit before speaking. "The Wereall guard who was there earlier isn't there now."

"Did you see the cells?" Magda shivers at the memory.

Frankie had, while looking for the missing guard and any others who might be around.

"Hang on." Frankie scuttles back down the stairs and checks out the cells. Hmmm, occupancy looks to be one hundred percent. Each of the cells that honeycomb the inside of the fortress is home to some unfortunate. Her dad's there somewhere, she can sense it. Five levels of cells puts the inmate population conservatively at around five hundred. That's either a lot of bad guys, or a lot of innocents.

Her gaze sweeps the grim interior from side to side. She's focusing on a nearby cell, when Zane joins her. Rather than an orange jumpsuit, the prisoner is wearing what looks to be a bespoke suit, complete with a surprisingly white shirt and a long red tie. It looks like her theory of the Garnet family getting rid of their business adversaries to this place is right. This isn't to say some so-called business moguls didn't deserve to be here.

Rather than be a noisy place, the prison is whisper quiet with all the prisoners floating in their allotted cells as though asleep. This is of some comfort to Frankie who's worried she'll find her dad a gibbering wreck.

Zane gasps, grabs Frankie and forces the pair of them back up the stairs. Only once they're sitting on the roof, does she notice how pale he his. "What is it?"

"It was Mimi. And she looked exactly the same as I remember." Frankie finds consolation in him shaking like a wet dog, showing he's not looking back on his time with the woman favorably.

"Did she see you?"

"I don't think so. I can't sense her."

"What do you mean?"

Turns out if Mimi wanted to get her claws into him again, he'd know all about it.

"The date wasn't as pleasant as the dreams had been, that's for sure." Zane shudders in remembrance.

"Hang on a second. If she's back looking how she did when you were dating, then she must know you're here."

Zane smacks his hand into the stone roof of the keep. "Blast it. I hadn't thought of that. We'll need to be the lookout for her."

"Don't you worry about that, I will be." Frankie sincerely hopes this is the case, because if she runs into the woman down in the *Keep*, she's not holding back. And if her magic doesn't work against the demon, she knows her Jeet Kune Do moves will. It must be something that shows on her face.

"Frankie, I don't want you going near her. There's no telling what she can do to you. She's evil, pure evil."

Frankie holds her hands up in surrender, hoping Zane doesn't spot she's got a couple of fingers on one hand crossed.

. . .

It takes all of twenty minutes to come up with a rough-and-ready plan. Even Dex is able to add a couple of good ideas to the mix. He really is rather devious when he puts his mind to it.

Able to perform magic in this dimension, Frankie double checks the magical safety net she's cast around them. It's one that has them pretty much bullet-proof. Not that the Werealls appear to be armed with anything other than brute strength and cunning. Frankie binds herself to Dex magically, over and above the natural connection they already have. This way there's no chance of losing him in the mayhem that is bound to ensue. While she'll be able to move away from him, she'll always know where he is and be able to bring him to her.

They're ready to start inching their way back down the staircase when the rock mirage falters and then disappears. There's nothing between them and the inside of the *Keep.*

The question is, can the half dozen guards strategically placed around the top level of the *Keep* see them?

Frankie doesn't wait to find out if the guards can see them; instead levitating all the guards as one and flinging them far out into the sea.

Turning to the others, Frankie finds them shocked. Magda appears lost for words and Zane is shaking his head slowly. Even Dex has his mouth hanging open. "Relax would you? I put a ward around them so the sharks won't get them and made sure they had a soft landing." There's no way Frankie wants blood on her hands, although she may draw the line with Mimi Merriweather, she-devil extraordinaire.

12

With the first wave of guards cooling off in the gray sea, there's no need to slither down the stone steps. Instead they make short work of racing down the first flight to the top level, finding the prison empty, but for inmates.

With no-one to stop them, they rush around the walkway of the top level looking at each of the prisoners in turn. Frankie hopes she's able to recognize her dad from old family photos because there aren't any names posted outside the cells.

Of note is how many of the prisoners on the top level are in suits and ties. This marks them as being those captains of industry stupid enough to cross paths with the Garnet family.

They're on the ground level before she finds a

prisoner she thinks is her father due to his flaming red hair. The strangest thing is that he doesn't appear a day older than he does in the photos she has of him. Him wearing a shirt and tie she can't even see if he's wearing one of the family amulets. Even though her mom always said the amulet she wears once belonged to her father, it wouldn't be the first time her mom lied to protect her.

"Dad?" Although Frankie has said this as quietly as she can, it sounds thunderous in the cavernous space. However the man floating before her doesn't move, or even open his eyes, it's as if he's trapped where he is. Of course! Courtesy of a lazy wave of her hand, Frankie removes the concealment and silence spells. However with the Werealls apparently able to smell a hot dog at 100 pages, she isn't risking removing her special deodorant spell. Once again, she whispers "Dad?"

This time his eyes snap open and he looks directly at her before breaking into a wide grin. "Frances?"

How is Frankie supposed to talk to someone who looks to be the same age as she is? Even calling him dad has felt a little weird.

Magda pushes hard against the invisible force that fronts the cell. "How the 'eck do we free 'im?"

Zane then throws himself bodily at the force

field, bouncing off it and land in a heap on the ground. "I'm not sure." He gets to his feet and starts exploring every inch of the gray granite that faces the cell. "There has to be some way of triggering the release."

Even Magda and Dex are engaged in searching for anything that resembles a switch of any kind.

While there aren't bars, the front of the cell is as solid as a sheet of bullet proof glass.

"There has to be a way." Frankie reaches out to touch the force field expecting to feel something solid under her hand. Instead her fingers go straight through. It's something that even surprises her dad, because as soon as she does so, he drops to the ground with a grunt.

Unfortunately after twenty years of not using his legs, he's as weak as a baby Wereall and stays exactly where he's fallen. The force field broken, Zane enters the cell and picks her dad up. The ease with which he does so telling Frankie her dad must be lighter than she is herself. The state her dad is in will make it both easier and harder for them to get him back through the caving system, and safely home.

Frankie starts to speak to her dad for the second time in twenty years, but stops. By craning her ear toward the middle of the *Keep*, she's able to hear voices, lots of them. "We're about to have company."

Zane hefts her dad to get him in a more comfortable position. "We're going to need a diversion, and fast."

"Take care of him." Frankie doesn't bother with any further explanation, instead transporting herself up to the top of the *Keep*. She knows what she's about to do will have both good and bad consequences. But this will be as good a way as any of keeping the Wereall guards busy. Busy enough to keep them occupied while she and the others make good on their escape through the cave. It's there they'll be helpless, with her magic once again taken from her. The fewer guards they encounter in the caverns, the better.

She doesn't give herself any more time to think about it. She bounces on her toes a couple of times to get her muscles moving and she sprints around the walkway. As she goes, she runs her hand across the force field of each and every cell. The prisoners drop one-by-one to the ground of their cells, the air filling with their grunts and cries. She manages to complete the top two levels before the central courtyard is flooded with Wereall guards. Wonky wands, she'd been hoping for more time than this.

She makes a promise right there that if they get out of here; she's coming back for anyone else who shouldn't be locked up in this awful place. Let's see the Garnet family rake in the money after their fiscal slaves are freed.

Back in her dad's cell, Frankie puts the concealment and silence spells back in place, this time including her father. She then gets the group to huddle together and transports them to the mouth of the cave. Not that they're free and clear.

The entrance is crammed wall-to-wall with more guards. This is exactly what she'd be hoping to avoid. Even with them being invisible like they are, there isn't so much as an inch free to sneak through.

Frankie throws an immobilis spell in their direction. It fails spectacularly. Okay, so magic can't cross the invisible barrier. "Magda, are you okay to carry him while Zane and I crack a few heads together?"

"He is so light, it will be easy." True to her words, Magda takes her dad off Zane, freeing him to help Frankie clear the way.

"Dex, are you ready to do like we practiced?"

Even though he nods rather than answer telepathically, she can tell his heart isn't in it. To be honest, she's in agreement that the guards are rather on the ferocious side of feral.

She, Dex and Zane then turn and face the solid wall of Wereall guards blocking their escape.

Rather than speak out loud, Frankie looks at Dex, sending her words of comfort to him silently *"Okay buddy, as we practiced. You're stronger than you think. Are you ready?"*

On receiving a squeaky *'yes'* in return, Frankie lifts the concealment spell on her small pal, revealing the small Jack Russell to the guards in the cave. It's something that has all of them growling ferociously and the hairs on the back of Frankie's neck at attention in response. On watching Dex shoot forward into the cave and between the legs of the guard in the middle, Frankie couldn't be more proud. Not that the guard in the middle seems concerned, even breaking into loud laughter. Now behind the guard, Dex spins around and assumes his famous attack pose erring on the side of cute for effect. Exactly as they've practiced.

The guard whose legs he's shot between doesn't bother turning and is still laughing when Dex jumps and chomps down hard on his posterior. He's not so amused after this, twisting and turning in an effort to free his left cheek of fifteen pounds of determined terrier.

Now it's the other guards who are laughing, although not at Dex but rather at their comrade. It's then that Zane and Frankie wade into them. By the time Frankie has taken out her third guard, she senses they're not used to fighting invisible opponents. Sure they're big and buff, most likely from hours spent pumping iron rather than actually doing anything with it. She almost feels mean, almost.

She's run out of guards to pummel when Zane knocks the last one unconscious. Frankie isn't sure what Zane is about frisking the guard as though he's going to lift the guy's wallet. Then he stands tall, holding up what looks like a garage door remote.

"Of course, the lights. Right, let's get the heck out of here."

The remote safely stuffed in Zane's pocket, he Magda and Frankie set about tying up the guards to keep them exactly where they are. Thankfully there are a lot of belts and shoelaces to hand, making this a reasonably easy procedure.

Zane and Frankie are looking at the dog pile at one side of the cave when he puts his hand on her shoulder before she can start into the depths of the cave.

"Hang on, we need to seal the way so we can't be followed by the others."

"I can't perform magic in here and we don't want to block the way completely."

"There are others who shouldn't be there." Her dad's words are so soft that it's only the echo of the cave that's allowed Frankie to hear them.

"Yeah, what my dad says." Frankie savors the words 'my dad' before carrying on. "We can't block the entrance."

"You can if you leave the cave."

Frankie's shocked by Zane's words. However, if it means there's a chance her dad and the others will get away, then that's the way it's gotta be.

Frankie hugs Magda and her dad, before picking up Dex and squeezing him tight. She then puts him back down carefully. Finally she walks back to Zane and pulling him close, kisses him as though she'll never get another chance. She doesn't think she will. Not that this will stop her doing what she has to, to protect those she loves.

Without a backward glance she leaves them and before she can stop herself or think it through, she throws a hex at the mouth of the cave. Only after it's in place does she see her error. It's one that will stop everyone entering, not just the We-reall guards. This includes all the prisoners in the

Keep who have no right being locked up. Now stuck here the same as those poor unfortunates, Frankie drops to the nearest rock and gives into her tears. She's been so close to having a family again. So very close.

The flow of tears has abated somewhat when someone wraps their arms around her from behind, dragging her into a tight embrace. Frankie doesn't hold on to any of the hurt or pain she's feeling. She slams her elbow into the solar plexus of whoever it is before snapping her head back in a move designed to break noses. The arms fall away allowing her to scramble to her feet and face her attacker.

"Zane? What on earth are you doing here? You can't be here! You can't. I blocked the cave." Frankie gives into her tears again. Here she was thinking she'd saved those she loves from hurt. On looking up and seeing Dex, Magda and her dad now right behind the Nautilus, Frankie loses it.

"What the heck is going on? I hexed the mouth of the cave to keep you safe. You should have stayed where you were. You shouldn't have been able to leave."

Zane scratches the back of his head and shifts his feet awkwardly.

Rusty cauldrons, looks like her magic has failed yet again.

"We couldn't leave you behind, *Pumpkin*," says her dad, from the safety of Magda's arms. "Not here. Not in this place." That Zane smiles at her dad calling her *Pumpkin* isn't lost on Frankie. He's one to judge, calling her Shortcake all the time. Frankie also knows the nickname her dad has used sounds familiar, not that her mom ever called her by it. Could it be that she remembers being called it after all this time?

"We all leave, we all stay." Magda's tone is emphatic even if her broken English has the message a little vague.

Dex winds himself around her ankles before looking up at her. *"I can never leave you. I'd die without you."*

Frankie isn't sure if he's stating a fact or being dramatic, but she bends her legs and pats her thighs. He jumps up and both of them take comfort in their closeness.

Zane, who's looking over her shoulder, draws in a huge lungful of air, "Best you lift that hex so we can get out of here."

They turn as a group and run toward the cave, slamming into an invisible force-field that has them staggering back.

"Are you kidding me?" Frankie smacks her hand against the wall of magic that's all that stands between them and freedom.

Zane turns to check out the location of the Wereall guards. "You better lift it, Shortcake, we don't have much time."

"But, you don't understand. I can't lift it. I didn't want to be tempted."

Magda lowers her dad to the ground although she keeps hold of him so he stays upright. "We are stuck 'ere?"

Zane runs his hands through his hair, not once, but twice. "Oh Frankie, what have you done?"

Even knowing his question is rhetorical, Frankie answers him anyway. "Screwed up?"

"Frances, it might be best if you at least move us somewhere. Other than here that is."

Her dad's expression matches that of Zane, and Frankie doesn't need to turn to know the marauding horde of Wereall guards is closer than ever.

Not that this stops her from twisting around. "Do you think that's all of them?" She sure hopes so. Frankie clutches onto Dex with one arm and holds the other wide, encouraging the others to stand close to her.

. . .

Looking around the cramped confines of the gray-walled cell, her dad is the first to speak. "I never thought I'd be seeing this place again."

Frankie grins at the horrified group before her. "Come on, let's lock all the doors and clear the vermin out of this place."

It's then that understanding dawns on Zane's face, and he's soon grinning as broadly.

Magda is left protecting her dad, while Zane, Frankie and Dex leave in search of any doors to the outside. There are just two and these are soon secured with heavy steel bars. Frankie even hexes the bejinkers out of them to make doubly sure no one is going to break in on them.

The three of them then search the fortress a floor at a time disabling any guards they come across. In lieu of anything to tie them up with, Frankie sends the lot of them off to *swim with the fishies* as Magda would say. With this many guards raining down on the choppy waters, she doubts there'll be a shark staying around to taste what's on offer. Not that they can with her 'no-chew' wards in place.

There's one place they haven't searched, the room at the top of the tallest tower in the stronghold. That this will be home to the Commander of the Werealls Frankie takes as a given. This is also where Frankie expects to find Mimi. Frankie stands at the bottom of the final flight of stone stairs and puts her finger to her lips to stop any conflab.

"Dex, why don't you go back downstairs and protect Magda and my dad?"

He plonks himself down on the unforgiving floor, determined to remain. *"I'm staying with you."*

"Sorry, that's not happening." Frankie waves her hand, and he disappears. Not that this keeps him quiet, with her easily able to hear him grumbling telepathically.

"Shhh, I need to concentrate."

Now it's all down to Zane and Frankie. She knows Dex isn't happy about her sending him back down to the ground floor. She, on the other hand, is a lot happier knowing he's safe.

Frankie mimes her fingers climbing stairs and gets a nod from Zane. Before they can start, he puts his hand under her chin and lifts her face before placing a chaste kiss on her lips. He's then all business again, although it takes Frankie a little longer to be ready to storm the tower.

Climbing the stairs as quietly as they can, they wait a beat before both kicking the large wooden door as near to the lock as they can. It slams open smashing hard against the wall and letting them know it hadn't actually been locked.

Instead of William as Frankie's been expecting. She's looking at the woman she'd seen when she first crossed the crevasse. Not that she stays looking that way, with her locks immediately changing from platinum blonde to brunette and her body shimmering into an even more voluptuous shape.

Hmmm, if this is what the succubus knows appeals to Zane, why on earth is he interested in her? Frankie couldn't be more different if she tried.

"Zane darling, I was hoping it would be you."

The woman doesn't bother getting up from the large bed of furs she's reclining on. That she's decked out like a lingerie model right down to a pair of silver stiletto heels has Frankie grinding her teeth. Sensible shoes they most definitely are not. "Why don't you send your little friend back downstairs so we can catch up on old times?" She then pats the mattress beside her in clear invitation.

Frankie stays right where she is and heaven help Zane if he tries to get her to leave. It will not be pretty. Frankie crosses her arms over her chest, worried Zane will see how lacking she is in this department compared to Mimi. "Does the elder member of the Garnet family know you're two-timing him with one of those beasts?"

"No. And nor will he once I've disposed of you." So conversational is Mimi's tone that it's almost as if she hasn't just threated Frankie's life.

Right, no more *Miss Nice Girl*. Frankie stomps over to the bed, jumps up on it — bouncing Mimi in a most satisfying manner — and flings the windows above the bed, wide open. She takes great delight in the ice laden air that whisks into the room, turning the skin of the succubus from satin smooth to mottled and covered in goosebumps. The demon needs to dress to suit the weather.

Oh, Frankie is going to take great pleasure in this.

13

Frankie isn't sure who gets the biggest shock. Zane that she's actually followed through or Mimi who hasn't realized Frankie can perform magic while at the *Keep*.

Zane, who's hanging out of the window, turns to her. "Do you think she can swim?"

"To be honest, I don't care."

"Did you hit her with the shark repellent spell?"

Frankie nods. Then on seeing the disappointment on Zane's face, gives consideration to lifting the protection. Much as Mimi has left a trail of destruction behind her, Frankie doesn't want that demon's blood marring her conscience or her soul. An ice cold dunking will do, for now.

They're about to head back down to her dad's cell when they become aware of pounding. A quick search of the room doesn't reveal any likely causes, so they move to the other rooms that make up the top floor. Only on entering the bathroom do they find the source.

Frankie flings open the doors of the large armoire while Zane stands at the ready to take care of any thumping that might be required. On seeing the state of the man tied up in the cupboard, they know there isn't any chance of retaliation. He's trussed up in enough rope to having him resembling a Thanksgiving ham. Although the apple stuffed in his mouth as a make-shift gag smacks more of a suckling pig.

It's only after she's removed the apple that recognition hits Frankie. "William?"

He confirms this with a brief nod. "Can you please untie me?"

Frankie's already working on the first knot, when Zane puts his hand on top of hers. "Not so fast, Shortcake."

"We can't leave him like this." Maybe it's that Frankie's mesmerized by those chocolate brown eyes? Whatever it is, the need to help him is overwhelming. She swats Zane's hand away and moves to work on another knot.

"Reveal yourself!" Zane's voice is thunderous and loud enough that Frankie fumbles with the knot.

On seeing what it is that's tied up, she drops the rope and stumbles back. Not that the Wereall has revealed himself as a conglomeration of animal body parts. Rather she's looking at a man way older than her granddad. That he's leering at her with pink-rimmed rheumy eyes like she's a piece of prime rib has her itching to smack him.

The old guy doesn't want to answer Zane's questions. Frankie hits him with a compelling spell that has him spilling the beans, franks, and even dessert about what's been happening on the island. Sounds as if the Werealls aren't entirely innocent when it comes to the prisoners put there by the Garnet family. That Mimi has been instrumental in the set-up is a given and something William confirms. No seduction has been necessary in this instance.

Rather than transport them straight back to her dad's cell, Frankie and Zane walk down the stairs, giving themselves a chance to process all they've learned.

Frankie stops to peer out another window. "Isn't it just typical that this would all be down to greed?"

"That and power. They're great motivators for some."

The disgust currently making itself at home on Zane's face tells Frankie he's thinking about Mimi. Frankie's in agreement, although her matching sneer of disgust is more to do with Mimi consorting with the lecherous old man upstairs.

As they pass another window, Frankie has another peek outside. "I think that's all of them."

Zane stands next to her and together they watch the guards swarming the main door of the *Keep*. "They must be using a battering ram."

"Let's get the heck out of here." As to how they're going to break through the hex, she's placed on the mouth of the cave, Frankie has no idea. Maybe there's another way in?

"We'll still have to work out how to get back into the caves."

"Yes, thanks for that, Captain Obvious."

Even though Frankie knows she's being snarky, them effectively being trapped on the island, is all down to her and it doesn't sit well.

Instead of walking down the rest of the way, Frankie transports them to just outside her dad's cell. She knows Dex is pleased to see her even though she's been giving him regular telepathic updates that she's okay.

Magda and her dad also appear relieved to see them back.

Frankie's also pleased to see her dad is better dressed for the cold weather. As well as the clothes he had on before, he's wearing a coat, gloves and a hat.

Magda tilts her head in Frankie's dad's direction. "Dex looked after him while I went to find the clothes."

Frankie smiles her thanks before turning to Zane. "Are you able to lift my dad?"

The Nautilus doesn't need to be asked twice and is soon standing holding her dad, ready for them to depart.

Frankie doesn't even bother transporting them to the mouth of the cave. Instead they arrive at the far end of the island, well away from the *Keep* and the cave entrance.

Magda looks around, clearly confused. "We are in wrong place, yes?"

Rather than be confused, Dex looks hungry, with a lot of lip licking going on.

Frankie hunkers down next to him, trying to working out what it is he's staring fixedly at. "What is it, Dex?"

"I smell sausages."

"Sausages?" Because the others are unable to

hear the small dog, Frankie's query has them all looking at her as if she's lost the plot. "Dex says he can smell sausages."

Zane adjusts his hold on her dad. "Lead the way, my young friend."

"What a clever pup," says her dad, breaking his silence.

Dex takes the lead, and they clamber over the rocks until they're standing facing a tank-sized boulder. Dex keeps sniffing the ground until his nose runs into the side of this beast. That he doesn't move from the spot lets them know he's found the source. Unfortunately there isn't a frypan in sight.

Frankie knows her familiar well enough to know his nose is always spot on. Especially when it comes to baked goods and processed meats. Frankie hunkers down next to him and examines the wall. There's nothing but rock, so far as she can see.

Her amulet has other ideas, lighting up and sending a beam to a spot right next to Dex's nose. It's bright enough that he jumps back, rolling a couple of times in his eagerness to get out of the way. Following a quick check to see if he's okay, Frankie returns to watching the rock. If she wasn't looking at it as closely as she is, she wouldn't have seen the subtle change that takes place. Putting her palm against the rock, Frankie isn't altogether surprised when her hand goes straight through.

"Come on." Unsure if it's just her who's able to pass through this mirage, Frankie places herself half in and half out of the rock. She then stays there while the others pass through, disappearing as they do so. Only after they're all safely through does she follow them.

Not that she can go far, with all of them jammed inside what looks to be a store cupboard of some kind. If it wasn't for the light streaming in under the bottom of the door, they'd be in pitch black. Eventually Frankie is able to make everyone out. She's about to speak, but Magda puts her finger to her lips, before tapping her ear twice and pointing at the door.

A brief wave of Frankie's hand and there's another shield of silence around them. Here's hoping this one actually works. To be on the safe side, Frankie's made it strong enough they could scream and shout and no-one in the next room would be able to hear.

Frankie looks at the door and then the others. "Is it locked?"

Zane shakes his head. "We were waiting for you."

Magda tilts her head toward the door. "We 'ave no way of knowing where it leads."

Her father doesn't say anything. Even in the half-light Frankie can see his eyes are closed and his mouth partly open. She needs to get him back to Stanley, and fast.

"Magda, are you okay to take my dad again?"

While the energy vamp is stronger than most men, she's nowhere near as strong as Zane. She also doesn't have anywhere near his fighting skills. The woman therefore shows no reluctance to play the part of a nursemaid with the transfer taking place without so much as a word.

Squeezing between the others, Frankie faces the door, with Zane at her side and Dex right behind them. Zane gently grasps the handle and turns it as slowly and quietly as he can.

Frankie looks at him and mouths, "One, two, three, go!"

Without making a sound, Zane swings the door wide. They're about to storm in as a group when they see the room is empty. Not that it's barren. The place is done up like a medieval banqueting hall complete with a large oak table that's set for a meal. If she didn't know better, Frankie would even think someone was expecting them.

It takes her dad's stomach gurgling for Frankie to realize she's also ravenous. Magda carefully puts her dad down on the chair at the end of the table. It being a carver, there's less chance of him sliding off this one. Zane meantime jams another heavily carved chair under the handle of the one other door in the room locking them in, and everyone else out.

Safe from interruption, Frankie walks over to the large wood-burning oven that's built into a chimney breast that dominates the room. It's time to help themselves to those sausages Dex is drooling over. The heat being generated by this monster and it doesn't take long before hats, scarves and gloves are being removed and jackets unzipped. It's a lot warmer in the banqueting hall than it had been outside or in the *Keep* itself.

Half an hour later and despite them all having eaten well, Frankie gets up and walks back to the large oven. The Goddess knows when their next meal will be along.

Taking a cloth off the bench, she swings open the large iron door, and is assailed with a wave of heat. "Does anyone want more sausages or hash browns? Remember this might be it for a while."

She's met with a chorus of yeses, with even her dad sounding stronger than he had earlier.

By the time they're replete, there isn't so much as a crumb left. And, with them knowing the food was more than likely for the guards doesn't fill any of them with remorse.

Putting the last plate in an apron-front sink the size of a baby's bath, Frankie rinses her hands under the tap. While the breakfast might have been for the guards, she knows they won't be the poor shmucks stuck with tidying up. Her mom would haunt her if she left the place a mess. On receiving a nod of approval from her dad, Frankie knows she's done right.

Zane simply shakes his head in bewilderment at her domesticity. "Can we go now?"

Only after they've shrugged back into their jackets and stuffed hats, gloves and scarfs into pockets do they stand ready to leave the room. The chair removed from under the door handle, they follow the same procedure as earlier. Zane and Frankie are up front, followed by Dex and finally Magda with her dad.

This time rather than finding a banqueting hall, they exit into an enormous cavern, central to which is something straight out of a sci-fi movie. The machine is the size of some apartments

Frankie has lived in and bristles with lights, buttons and levers.

It can be only one thing, the *Syphonia*.

While it's important that they get out of here, it's also important for her dad's powers to be given back to him. Only trouble is how on earth are they supposed to do that? It would take a degree in advanced electronics to figure out how to make this beast work. Last time Frankie checked, this wasn't listed on her résumé and she doubts she's alone in this.

There's no way they can wing it either, not without potentially scrambling her dad's magic, or worse, his brain.

"I expected you before now."

All of them to a man, woman and dog, spin to face the new arrival. Even if she hadn't spoken, they'd know the Wereall was female, with her fluffiness and size firmly labeling her as one of the gentler sex. While the male Werealls appear to favor killer animals, the woman before them is obviously lower down the food chain. That she's standing calmly with her hands clasped in front of her also says she's not a threat. Not that her hands stay there for long, with one of them straying to her throat.

Frankie can tell by how the woman's gaze follows them as they move that she can see them as clearly as they can see each other. Hexed hedgehogs, Frankie forgot to reinstate the concealment spell when they left the *Keep*.

On thinking back to where it was she reinstated the spell of silence, Frankie realizes they might have a problem. She then notices the Wereall woman has pushed the fur at her neck to one side. It's this that allows Frankie to see the amulet hanging there. It's the same shape as that around her own neck although Frankie isn't close enough to see if the runes are a match.

Hmmm, could it be that Calico Jack and Anne pilfered the amulets off the Werealls? It wouldn't surprise Frankie as her piratical relatives don't appear to think anything of stealing if it suits their needs, or simply for a tidy profit.

The humanoid kitten wringing her hands, tells Frankie she's nervous without need of words. Her voice then quavering when she speaks again, doubly confirms it. "We do not have much time. The *Syphonia* is ready for the transfer." She delicately sniffs the air before continuing. "We must hurry. Time is not our friend."

Now this, Frankie hasn't been expecting. Why would the woman be willing to help them? Not keen on plugging her dad into this machine when it could be a trap, Frankie walks over and puts her hand on the woman's shoulder. This stops her getting any closer to the machine. "Why are you helping us?"

The woman's shoulders slump proving beyond doubt she can hear them. Frankie isn't surprised by this as she's already worked out that her putting the spell in place when they were already inside the cave had been a pointless exercise. "Because this, this is not who we are. The Werealls keep the peace. We don't imprison the innocent." That her gaze swings to Frankie's dad after she says this, confirms he's one of the wrongly imprisoned.

At first Frankie takes the woman at her word even allowing her to continue toward the machine. But something's off. It would appear her gut instinct works on this side of the crevasse too. "There's got to be more to it than this."

The woman doesn't answer immediately, concentrating on the dials and levels on the control board of the humongous machine. Not that she makes a move to change any of them from their current settings. "Her fur, it is not natural. No-one has fur that soft or shiny. She has taken my mate from me. He is blinded by her beauty."

Zane stands on the other side of the woman. "You mean Mimi Merriweather?"

"Yes! This is all her doing."

If the woman is an enemy of Mimi the succubus, then she's definitely a friend of theirs. Frankie allows her dad to sit in the large chair positioned in front of the machine. Not that she's entirely comfortable watching the Wereall woman strapping him in. She has to fight hard to stand still on seeing what looks like an old-school hairdryer dropped into place over her dad's head.

Her dad secure, the woman returns to the control panel and after hovering over a couple of levers and a few dials, places her hand on a large green button. She's about to push it, when the double doors at the end of the cavern slam open.

Standing in the middle of the open space is Mimi Merriweather, dripping wet and mad as hell. Carefully pulling a piece of seaweed from her long dark tresses, she tosses it to one side.

"Selena, don't you dare."

But it appears the Wereall woman does dare. After snarling at the demon, the woman dramatically slams her hand down on the button. The transfer of power starts immediately.

14

Mimi flies across the room screaming like a banshee, her hands outstretched. There isn't a chance in Hades Frankie is going to allow her to stop the reversal. Her dad is getting his powers back, and she doesn't care what she needs to do to keep the transfer going. Frankie jumps between Selena and Mimi and stands with feet apart, arms hanging loose at her sides.

This madness stops here.

Unfortunately for Mimi, she takes Frankie's 'at ease' stance at face value and doesn't slow. Unable to use her powers in the cave, Frankie isn't too concerned. She knows handing the succubus her derriere on a tray is going to be so much more fun.

Even without turning, Frankie knows the Wereall female behind her is freaking out; her animal-like whimpering says it all. Frankie does her best to ignore what this does to her spine. Instead she concentrates on Mimi, counting off the beats until she needs to spring into action.

Three... two... one...

Rather than try to stop Mimi, Frankie helps her to keep going, even putting her foot out to the side. This playground maneuver sends the woman into a sprawled heap of silver heels and high-end lingerie. Not giving her time to get up, Frankie throws herself on top of the evil cow. "Selena, you keep the transfer going while I take care of this trash."

Frankie's got the upper hand until Mimi is suddenly flooded with power. So far as Frankie knows, this shouldn't be possible in the caving system. Where the demon is getting it from, she has no idea. The succubus is strong enough that she's more than a match for Frankie, even without martial arts training. While Frankie could call on Zane to help, it's not in her nature. There's also no way she wants her boyfriend — there she's said it — anywhere near this woman.

Frankie's close to being overpowered by Mimi when she becomes aware of energy flickering at the edge of her soul. It's not from Mimi, it's from the machine. If she could just reach out psychically and draw on it. Her concentration is thrown when a stiletto heel spikes her calf muscle.

Owww, that hurt.

Even having elbowed Mimi in the forehead in response, Frankie doesn't think she can hold out much longer. Things change in a heartbeat. Again sensing the energy flickering around her, Frankie's tapped into it before she's even aware of doing so. Only question is, will it affect the transfer to her dad?

By grabbing a handful of Mimi's silky hair, Frankie easily holds the demon's head still so she can stare the woman in the eye. "Give it up. You have been beaten."

"I never give up!" Gone is the face of a beauty queen. The visage Frankie's looking at has more in common with the ugliest Halloween mask in the shop. Sheesh, talk about the makeover from hell. It takes all Frankie's nerve to keep hold of the woman.

Her preference is to let go of the greasy gray locks and scrub her hands with washing up liquid until they squeak. It also gives Frankie an insight into what Mimi has been using some of her accumulated power for. Sheesh, Frankie's heard of vanity projects before, but this takes the biscuit.

"Selena, how much longer before my father is powered up?"

Frankie looks up to find her dad watching her with pride. That he's standing on his own is a good sign. "It's all good *Pumpkin*. I'm... back to my old... I'm as good as new."

Frankie scrambles to her feet, all without letting go of Mimi's lank hair. "Magda, are you able to help me here?"

"It will be my pleasure."

Between them, the two women drag the kicking and screaming she-devil over to the once again vacant chair in front of the *Syphonia*. Strapping her in is made easier once Frankie's dad springs in and helps. This freaks the heck out of Frankie. "Get away from her, dad! She'll latch onto you."

"Hah, like the fiend hasn't tried in the past. I'm immune to her charms. My love for your mother makes sure of that. It's why she had to use this place to suck my powers from me."

Frankie, who's holding onto one of Mimi's arms, tightens her grip. She shoves the woman back into the upholstered seat, snapping a metal bar into place over her wrist. Her hands free she pulls Mimi's head around so she can look her in the eye. "Is this true?"

"I... Need... Power!"

Frankie isn't sure if Mimi is talking about right now, or in general. She's about to ask the demon to clarify this, when the woman continues.

"Your family has power."

Frankie's dad laughs briefly before snapping the ankle bar into place. It's a move that has him close to be kicked in the head. "But you couldn't access my powers, could you?"

Mimi confirms this and, like all baddies, then launches into a monologue.

It turns out that while researching the Bonny name Mimi stumbled across the Garnet family. Due to the family's ongoing bid to hold on to their multi-million dollar island resort by doing away with any Bonny they could find, it was a match made in hell. Especially so when Mimi discovered the island was also the site of one of the portals to the realm of the Werealls.

"The stupid old man who heads up the family really believes I'm in love with him." Mimi snorts in amusement. "The rich can be so delusional."

Zane moves to stand at Frankie's side. "Did you notice she's still talking in the present tense?"

Frankie nods, never taking her eyes off Mimi.

"All I had to do was smile at the elder Garnet and he had every one of this staff combing the island looking for the runes that would denote where the portal was."

Unable to listen to any more of the demon's ramblings, Frankie slams the metal hood over Mimi's skull-like head. Selena then wastes no time hitting a big red button on the control panel. That she does so with a lot of pomp and ceremony has Frankie and Magda both smiling.

Frankie is surprised at the speed of the process, with Mimi sucked dry in under a minute. There isn't a chance she could seduce a man with her ability to transform herself looking to be removed forever. So shriveled has she become there isn't even a need to remove the straps, with her skeleton-like limbs sitting loose in the constraints.

The woman's voice is pitched so low Frankie has to lean closer to hear her. "You should not have been able to perform magic in my realm."

"Your realm?" Frankie straightens to get herself away from breath that could definitely bring a man to his knees, and not in a good way. "Oh, get over yourself, would you?"

Frankie turns away from the succubus to look to her friends. Now that Mimi is taken care of and her dad powered up, they need to get out of here, and fast. She's not taken two steps toward them when a pair of boney hands clasp around her neck. Jinxed jellyfish, the woman is like a demon terminator.

On seeing Zane striding toward her, Frankie gasps out. "Don't you dare?"

Frankie puts her hands up and grabs Mimi's claws, snapping a couple of fingers off in the process. *Ooops.* It's then she senses power again, although this time it's coming from Mimi rather than the machine. It would appear the demon hasn't been sucked dry completely.

Frankie concentrates on the energy, gathering up every last ounce of it and taking it into herself. Unfortunately this isn't all she absorbs. And while knowledge is power, she'd rather not be privy to the memories swirling around inside her head. Not that these have her releasing the she-devil. Mimi needs to go and if Frankie has to succumb in the process, then it's a price she's willing to pay. The last drop of power taken from her, the demon collapses.

Not trusting outward appearances, Frankie nudges Mimi with her foot to see if she's truly gone. She's startled on seeing the demon's eyes snap open wide. Yep, terminator territory for sure.

Selena is having none of it. She takes to the husk of the succubus with a broom and keeps smashing away until all that's left is a pile of bone and ash. As violent as it's been, Frankie can't help but wonder if she wouldn't do the same if Mimi had got her claws into Zane again. She thinks perhaps she would.

With all of them, apart from Selena, aware that Mimi is dead; Magda has to forcibly take the broom off the Wereall for the annihilation to stop. "She is gone. You show us way out?"

It takes the woman a second to come back to her surroundings. "Oh, oh, yes. Follow me."

Unable to help himself, Dex trots over to the pile of smashed demon so he can sniff it before they leave. *"Yuck! Clean up in aisle 5."*

This time rather than staggering around in the dark, they follow the woman, with lights coming on at regular enough intervals for the way to be clear. Frankie has even recognized the strange yellow of the light that marks the exit to the island when she spots humanoid shapes approaching from the other direction.

Blast, it must be the guards they tangled with earlier. She was sure those knots would hold. It's either this or there's yet another entrance to the caving system.

Fortunately, Frankie and the others reach the yellow light before the guards. Frankie drops to her hands and knees in order to get her amulet as close as she can to the runes. It lights up immediately, and the cave is filled with the sound of graunching rock as the two sides of the crevasse split apart. After hurrying everyone through, Frankie brings up the rear exploding out into the humid heat of the island just before the rocks slam shut behind her.

Ignoring the others looking at her, Frankie stands in front of the crevasse. She places her hands on the rock and recites the spell from *The Book of Lore* that she's memorized.

Rocks remain and time stand still
this is my word, this is my will.
Sleep sound all those who have to stay
wake at my will another day.
A stasis on the world of Were
until such time as I declare.

The rock face under Frankie's hand shivers briefly before settling back down. On stepping back the only sign anything has changed is the set of runes carved into the granite directly in line with her amulet.

The hex in place, any Werealls in this world will be able to enter but won't be able to get back out again. Well, according to *The Lore of Craft*e that is. Kinda like one of those high-end cat-flaps which given the feline features of a lot of the We-realls is very appropriate.

"Come on *Pumpkin*, let's go home. Your mother and I have a lot of catching up to do."

And just like this Frankie's euphoria is smashed on the rocks of tragedy. She doesn't know how her dad is going to take it when he finds out his beloved wife is dead. Frankie's also unsure how she's going to break the news to him. All she knows is she's not doing it here.

Her father goes to transport them home, but Frankie holds her hand up. "Please, let me." She knows if her dad takes charge they'll end up back at her childhood home, shocking the new tenants and her dad in the process.

On hearing rustling from the ferns nearby, Frankie doesn't linger. Instead she grabs Dex, makes sure everyone else is in contact with her and then takes them all back to the *Pearl*.

On seeing their surroundings, her dad is confused. They're not in a huge rambling mansion in Portland as he's no doubt been expecting. Instead, they're on a boat. Zane and Magda leave immediately, knowing what it is Frankie has to do. This leaves Frankie, her dad and Dex, although even Dex looks like he'd rather be anywhere else.

"Dex, why don't you head on over to Magda's. I'm sure she'll have something delicious for you to eat." Even if it isn't that long since the small pup hoovered up a month's worth of sausages, he always has room for blueberry muffins.

On hearing Dex's toenails clattering down the dock, Frankie invites her dad to sit down on the bench seat that runs across the back of the cabin. As weird as it is to be sharing news like this with a man who is essentially a stranger, Frankie doesn't want to wait.

"Da.. dad. You've been gone a long time."

Her dad laughs. "I figured that out for myself, *Pumpkin*. You're all grown up."

"A lot has happened while you've been away."

He stills. "Don't tell me your mother remarried?"

Frankie shakes her head, unable to stop the tears that are rolling unhindered down her cheeks.

"Oh. What happened?"

By the time she's recounted the demise of his wife and her mom, he's got matching tears rolling down his own face. "And you say it's the Garnet family who are responsible."

Frankie sniffs out a yes.

"You know Mimi got me locked up so she could siphon my powers. I had a suspicion what was happening after she wouldn't take no for an answer. Your powers being what they were when you were little, I knew you'd be next. That's why I left instructions with your mom on what to do if I ever disappeared."

"It was you!"

"Don't go too hard on me, *Pumpkin*. You're alive and free aren't you?"

Frankie has to concede he's got a point, not that this has her any less miffed at all those years without powers. No wonder her mom hadn't wanted them living anywhere near other magical folk. This would have made it even harder to conceal the reason behind Frankie's lack of powers.

Her father, no longer able to remain seated, storms to his feet. "Those Garnets are going to pay for this."

"Trust me. I know," says Frankie, smiling for the first time since getting home. Even though she knows the Garnets were being used by Mimi, they aren't innocent either. While the demon had been after raw power, the family had been after money and that island. Actually make that her dad's island with him being the oldest *living* Bonny.

"Shame we can't go back in time and save your mother." His wistful tone has her smile slipping.

EPILOGUE

Frankie's heart swells with love and pride as she looks around *Magic Beans*. On one side of her sits Zane, on the other her dad. Anyone looking at the three of them would pick them as being around the same age. Nothing could be further from the truth. At her feet, curled up in a ball after scoffing three muffins, is Dex.

Stanley bangs a salt shaker on his table to get everyone's attention and for once, it works.

"Firstly, I'd like to welcome Colin Bonny to the Marina Coven. He's been gone a long time, so the more you can help him get up to speed, the better." That Stanley doesn't go into detail tells Frankie everyone already knows the full story. Witches gossip more than anyone she's ever met.

There's a polite smattering of applause, followed by a few witches nearby lifting their coffee in a silent toast. One thing her dad is having no trouble wrapping his head around, is today's coffee. When he'd been kidnapped, the king of coffee had been the filter variety. He's making up for lost time by working his way through *Magic Bean's* coffee menu. To stay he's a little on the fidgety side is an understatement.

The coven meeting follows the usual formula of news from other covens, followed by regular niggles. Frankie is glazing over as per usual, while Colin appears to be hanging on every word, seemingly unable to get enough of the day-to-day minutiae of coven life.

Her dad has told her that even while he's been in a state of suspension at *All Hallows Keep*, he's been aware of time passing. It's something that had him fretting, wondering if Frankie and her mom were okay. And even though it's been over twenty years since he saw his wife, this doesn't lessen his grieving.

The meeting wrapping up, Mac, the café owner, puts yet another coffee down in front of Colin Bonny. "This one's on the house."

"Dad, do you think you should? That'll be your fourth cup this morning."

"This is the last for the day, I promise. I had a bit of trouble sleeping last night."

Frankie isn't surprised. On escorting her dad to one of the spare cabins the night before, he'd been close to flying, without a broom.

Frankie's walking across the carpark with Zane and Colin and marveling at how much colder it is than when they'd left for the island. Hard to believe she was padding around in bare feet a mere day or so back. She's thinking about transporting herself, Dex and her dad back to the *Pearl* when Stanley catches up with them.

It's this that has her waving her hand in the air and changing her hoodie out for her puffer jacket. She then sorts out something similar for her dad who's not dressed for the weather, either. If it wasn't for the fact Frankie had transported them to the café in the first place, they would have realized how cold it is as soon as they stepped onto the deck of the *Pearl*. Zane as usual is fully prepared.

"Colin, if it's alright, I'd like to check out your health. Best to see there's no lasting damage to your powers."

Her father nods in agreement to this. "I think that's a very good idea."

They continue onto Pier 51, stopping next to the dock that leads to the *Annie*.

"Colin if you go on ahead, we'll catch up with you," says Stanley.

The coven leader then watches Frankie's father until he's standing next to the tugboat, before turning back to Frankie. "I think it's time you got your powers back too."

This statement has Frankie's thoughts in a whirl. Does Stanley mean ALL her powers, or just those he took from her as a form of punishment? Now that her dad is back can the jinx her mom placed on her finally be removed? All these questions whirring around in her brain, she has to shake her head to get herself back to the present.

"Dex, do you want to come with dad and me, or go with Zane?"

The small dog looks between Frankie and her boyfriend, eventually showing his decision by walking over and sitting next to the Nautilus. *"I'm still sleepy. I'll go with Zane."* It looks as though her dad wasn't alone in burning the midnight oil last night.

Frankie says goodbye to Zane with an innocent kiss on the cheek and a squeeze of his hand and then follows Stanley and her dad onto the *Annie*. She's last to arrive in the main cabin, with Stanley already running his hands over Colin's aura in the coven equivalent of an MRI.

While doing this, Stanley utters enough 'tsks' and 'hmmms' that Frankie is on tenterhooks before the examination is even over.

Frankie steps closer. "What is it?"

Stanley gives her a bright smile, maybe too bright. "It's nothing for either of you to worry about."

Colin sits himself down on the sofa. "If it's nothing to worry about, you won't mind telling me what you've found."

Stanley looks from father to daughter, obviously choosing his words. "I'll check Frankie out before I voice my conclusions."

Frankie steps closer to the coven leader. "Let's get on with it, then." To avoid being distracted by Stanley's hands waving around her, Frankie closes her eyes and slows her breathing. Not that it stays slow with Stanley soon back to all that 'tsking' and 'hmmming'.

Eventually Stanley's exclamations stop. "You can open your eyes."

On seeing Stanley sit in his favorite chair, Frankie joins her dad on the sofa. She gets the impression that sitting is going to be best for what they're about to hear.

Stanley looks first to Colin. "You're up to full power." A 'but' hangs in the air, waiting to make an appearance. It soon does. "But, your powers are different to any I've ever felt before. The person who operated the machine to give you your powers back at *All Hallows Keep*, who was it?"

Because Colin had been in a bit of a daze at the time, it's up to Frankie to fill in the gaps. She does this as thoroughly as she's able to, leaving nothing out.

"So you're saying the woman did nothing but press the green button? She didn't move any of the levers on the machine or push any of the other buttons?"

"Not that I saw. Mind you, she could have done that while we were eating breakfast." Thinking back on it, Frankie recalls something else. "I remember, she did hesitate a bit before she hit the green button."

"Hmmm, this could help explain things."

Colin and Frankie lean forward as one.

"Don't worry Colin you're up to full powers. As to who, or what, those powers belonged to originally..." Stanley breathes deeply before continuing; "I think I know, but I'll need to research it further before I can confirm it."

Colin sits back, absently grabbing Jojo, the Siamese, and dragging her onto his lap. "I must admit, my powers do feel different."

Frankie twists in her seat. "Is this why you haven't performed any magic?"

"I wasn't sure if I could. Or should."

Frankie knows exactly what he means. "Does it feel as though it could overpower you at any second? Like you're playing with fire and your hands are wet with gasoline? Explosive?"

Colin nods vigorously in response to every one of her observations.

"Is there something you need to tell us, *Pumpkin*?"

Frankie doesn't hesitate. Not that she's willing to spill absolutely everything. There are some things you need to explore yourself before you share. "Explosive is exactly how I've been feeling since I borrowed some energy from the machine in order to overpower Mimi."

Now it's Stanley's turn to sit forward in his seat. "You overpowered Mimi? But, that's not possible."

"Yep. And then we sucked every last ounce of power from her using that machine. The Wereall woman was particularly happy about that."

Frankie having told them everything she wants to, she falls silent. So what if she's left out the part about her dragging the last of the power swirling in the depths of the succubus? She's not even sure it's made any difference to her, so no need to talk about it now.

On hearing of the demise of Mimi, Stanley looks to be reflective. Whether this is because he's happy his ex-wife is gone for good, or he's mourning her demise, Frankie isn't able to tell, with the coven leader's expression guarded as it is.

Then he rouses himself and looks at her. "Would you like your powers back, now?"

"You took my daughter's powers? But, the restraining spell I instructed her mother to place on her means she shouldn't have any powers at all."

Rather than go into details as to how it is she's got some of her powers back, Frankie simply shrugs. "Dad, maybe it's time you removed that jinx on my powers."

"I don't know about that. The Garnet family is still at large. I don't think that's a good idea."

"But, Dad I need my powers!" Frankie knows she sounds like a whiney teenage brat who's just been told she can't use the car. She doesn't care. "I'm sick of being in danger because my powers have faltered, or failed me entirely."

"Perhaps it's best that your father and I discuss this."

Frankie stares hard at Stanley before speaking. "You're sending me from the room?" She's unable to stop the surge of anger at being summarily dismissed like this. It must be something that shows, with both men soon in possession of wands. Frankie's more than a little peeved to see the wand being held by her father is actually hers. What is it with the men in her life nabbing her wand like its common property?

Frankie has to force herself to calm down, speaking as evenly as she can. "If this concerns me, I have the right to stay."

For a moment, Frankie thinks Stanley is going to send her on her way despite her reasoned argument. On seeing his wand disappear, she breathes out in relief. She then holds her hand out for the wand her father is holding. Not that he hands it over.

"I'll need this to give you back your powers."

"So you're happy to give them back to me?"

"I think it better your own powers dominate rather than anything you've picked up along the way. Don't you?"

Hmmm, so it looks as though he's detected her anger isn't her own. Frankie hesitates. What if her old powers aren't as good as her new powers? "Will my witchy powers stop my, ah, other powers from working?"

On hearing a definitive 'no' from both men,

Frankie gives her dad the okay to remove the hold on her magic. "Do I need to stand, or anything?"

"Best if you simply sit back and relax. Relaxation is the key. I left instructions for your mom to put the jinx in place while you were asleep."

Frankie's leaning back and trying to relax when she remembers something. "It was the lullaby, wasn't it?"

Her father nods. This must be why the jinx on her powers has been faltering. Now her mom is no longer around to reinforce the spell it must have been slowly weakening. Frankie had always thought it odd her mom insisted on phoning her every night at bedtime. Now she can see it gave her mom the opportunity to sing the verse to her daughter that would reinforce the ward yet again.

"Come on, Frankie," says her dad, laying his hand gently on her shoulder. "Relax and we'll have this sorted in no time."

This has Frankie wound tighter than an eighties corkscrew curl and has to concentrate on her breathing to do as he's instructed. She finds closing her eyes and slumping back in the sofa helps too.

For a start nothing happens. Then Frankie becomes aware of power unfurling in her solar plexus. While it starts out slowly, the heat radiating from that one spot soon spreads throughout her body. It feels as though she's on fire. This isn't helped by the flickering sensation that fills her, with the power a living, breathing thing that's close to consuming her. Her eyes snap open, with the need to check she's not actually aflame, being overwhelming.

The biggest surprise is that while she's not actually alight, she's no longer sitting next to her dad on the sofa either. Instead she finds she's floating near the ceiling of the cabin and moving slowly in lazy circles. Panic is fighting her system for supremacy and it's only her dad's calm, 'Relax, everything is as it should be.' that stops her falling prey to it.

She's inspected the cabin's cross beams far more than she thought she ever would, before she floats back down and lands safely on the sofa next to her dad.

"It is done." Her dad hands her wand back to her, and she's surprised on holding it to feel her powers surge in response. A girl could get used to this.

"And you're both sure my new powers will still work? Being able to cast spells at *All Hallows Keep* when no-one else could, came in kinda handy."

"You performed magic at the *Keep*?" Stanley's

complexion pales, his voice when he speaks again, is weak. "Only Werealls are supposed to be able to perform magic while there."

Now it's Frankie's turn to lose color. "Maybe it's because it's Wereall magic?" Once again she's got her fingers crossed, musing on how often she's had to resort to this of late.

Stanley turns to Colin. "You aren't the first Bonny to ever be held at *All Hallows Keep*, are you?"

Her dad shaking his head fills Frankie with horror.

Frankie puts her hand on her dad's arm. "Is our other relative still there?"

"No thank goodness, she escaped a long time ago."

"She escaped?" Stanley crunches his forehead in concentration. "I don't remember hearing of any escapes."

Her dad grins broadly. "Yes, well, if it's a Wereall who helped you escape, it doesn't tend to get recorded."

Stanley's attention is firmly on Frankie's dad. "That can only mean one thing, surely?"

"From what I hear, it was a love match."

"I didn't think their kind were capable." Stanley taps *The Lore of Crafte* that's still on the coffee table. "Certainly there's nothing in the literature about this."

Frankie's been watching this back and forth and gone from wondering what they're on about to knowing exactly what they mean. "She was carrying his pup, kitten, litter or whatever, wasn't she, dad?"

Colin's wry smile is enough to confirm she's right.

Maybe those neighborhood bullies had been right on the money when they'd called her a mongrel. It does however explain how it is she was able to open the cells and walk through rock. Sheesh, at this rate, she and Dex are going to be bulk-buying flea treatments.

"Hang on. What relation is she to us?"

"She was my grandmother and your great grandmother."

Frankie clambers around in the family tree before deciding it must be one of Anne and Calico Jack's kids. "But that makes you part Wereall too. Why couldn't you perform magic while you were at the *Keep*?"

"Because I was drugged before I was taken there. Next thing I know all my powers have been sucked from me and I'm floating in that cell."

His talking about the cell has Frankie remembering the be-suited prisoners on the top levels. She looks between her dad and the coven leader. "We need to go back. We can't leave people locked up there just to keep the Garnets in business."

Stanley nods in agreement. "Yes. Unfortunately any recovery is going to have to wait. We won't be able to get the help we'll need until after the winter solstice has been celebrated."

Frankie sits up straight. "The solstice? That's ages away. We're not even half way through October."

"While it might feel as though you've been gone a day or so, in truth you've been gone for over two months of our time."

Frankie comes to a horrifying conclusion. "We missed Halloween?"

"You did indeed."

"Well that sucks." Frankie had been looking forward to this Halloween, her first living in a coven. She'd had big plans involving pumpkins. While Stanley is at a loss to understand her out of whack disappointment, her dad comprehends immediately.

"Awww, *Pumpkin*, we can celebrate your birthday any day."

It's her birthday falling on this most special of nights that is apparently part of the reason her dad's pet name for her is *Pumpkin*. Thank the Goddess her hair isn't as orange these days.

"It doesn't matter, Dad." And really it doesn't in the grand scheme of things. This will be his first Solstice since his release and so Frankie is going to make it the best Solstice ever. It might also take her mind off it being her first without her mom. Not that her mom had ever allowed them to celebrate the holiday, preferring to let it pass without acknowledgement.

And after the Solstice is over? Then she and as many witches, warlocks and whatever else they can round up are going back to *All Hallows Keep* and rescuing any prisoners who shouldn't be there.

FranKie B
Faerie Lights

ANDIE LOW

Squabbling Sparrows Press

1

Frankie looks around her cabin on the *Pearl*, the schooner she calls home. Part of her still can't believe she wrested it away from Captain Russell Garnet, the ghost haunting the Marina Coven. Not that getting rid of him was a walk in the marina, with her enchanted amulet the thing that kept her from dying. Well, that and good old-fashioned dumb luck.

After shaking her head to clear it of thoughts of the odious ghost and his uglier parrot, Frankie's once again in the present. The one thing she doesn't love today is her cabin, with it being about as festive as a supermarket that's in-between holiday promotions. A short window of opportunity to be sure, but she's managed it.

The lack of decorations is down to her late mom refusing to celebrate the Winter Solstice. Without anything to go on, Frankie hasn't got a clue what's involved. No inherited decorations, no inherited rituals. Nada. Add to this November disappearing due to a visit to a parallel universe and she hasn't had nearly enough time to get ready.

Frankie's trawling through *Wikipedia* intent on finding something she can work with, when Colin Bonny knocks and strolls into her cabin. He's the latest relative she's found, and the pick of the bunch to date. Moreover he's her dad, not that you'd know it to look at him. Like her he's tall, athletic and has fiery red hair, but his youthful looks often have him being mistaken for her brother. He's also the reason Frankie's agonizing over making this the best solstice, ever.

Unlike her mom, her dad's all for marking the solstice rather than letting it slide by unnoticed. He's never said as much, but there's no missing his whole face lighting up whenever anyone mentions the holiday, no matter how briefly.

His disappointment on scanning her cabin is enough to have Frankie feeling even guiltier about her lack of progress. After what her dad's been through in the preceding twenty years, she needs to go all out for him.

It's the least she can do when it was him being stuck in the parallel universe responsible for nixing November that allowed her to lead a normal life. Well, as normal as is possible for a witch who's been jinxed for most of her life. And a jinx that left her practically powerless at that.

Thank goodness she'd stumbled onto her own Mr Miyagi who'd taught her Jeet Kune Do the martial art developed by Bruce Lee. While her magic powers were known to let her down, her fighting skills never did. As a kid, it was these that were often all that was between her and a beating. More than once they'd pro-tected her from the scum in the low-end neighborhood that was all her mom could afford.

Frankie shakes her head to clear it of these less than pleasant memories. Unfortunately it's finding the present isn't too hot either. Her dad, obviously finding the lack of cheer in her cabin not to his lik-ing, has wandered off again.

He does that a lot these days, going from cabin to cabin as if searching for something. Too often she'll find him standing in the middle of an empty cabin, his expression pensive and his eyes glit-tering with unshed tears. While Frankie's had longer to come to terms with the death of her mom, seeing her dad choked up soon has her the same way.

What the pair of them need is a diversion of epic proportions. Here's hoping her new powers will allow her to decorate her cabin to within an inch of its life. She wants to make that solstice in-duced smile of her dad's a permanent feature.

She knows she can't aim too high, starting from scratch as she is. Perhaps something small, just to get things moving? Frankie scrolls down the screen on her phone until she finds something that will be perfect. A yule log. This should be easy enough. She just needs to include a fireplace in which the log can burn without taking out the *Pearl* in an inferno in the process.

A rough-and-ready *Pinterest* search and Frankie is faced with a myriad of images to choose from. After finding one particularly impressive specimen, she concentrates all her powers on manifesting something similar.

Home to the hearth
and heart of the home.
Bring me a yule log
and fire of my own.
Mark the Solstice
with wood and with bark

feeding the flame
to rid winter's dark.

A flourish with her hand and Frankie completes the spell.

Dex, her Jack Russell familiar, who's been lying on the end of her bed, is soon on his feet. He jumps onto the end of the huge log causing the plush reindeer antlers jammed on his head to bounce merrily. That his jaunty headwear smacks more of Santa than the solstice shows how desperate Frankie is.

"Wow! I take it you didn't mean to do this?"

Rather than speaking out loud, Dex has communicated with her telepathically. This is the remnant of a spell put on him by her late mom in hopes of stopping his incessant barking. Now all Frankie has to deal with is his incessant chatter. It used to be that everyone magical could hear Dex, these days it's just her. It's his tendency to tell anyone he meets everything he knows that has stopped her reinstating the spell. At least this way she can have *some* secrets.

Frankie looks at her familiar as he sniffs the log, and even though she doubts he's expecting a reply, she gives him one anyway. "Well, duh?" The small metal fireplace that barely holds one end of the merrily burning log simply isn't up to the task. For him to think she's done this on purpose is nonsense.

So focused is Frankie on the potential fire hazard, she isn't aware her dad has rejoined them until he speaks. "If it's okay with you?" He waves his hand at the overly large log and ridiculously small fireplace and reverses their sizes.

It's hearing tinny barking that alerts Frankie to Dex having been shrunk along with the yule log. "Any chance you can sort out Dex?"

"Sorry, *Pumpkin*."

Frankie's unable to stop the cringe at his use of this pet name. It was okay when she was a kid, not so much these days. There's also the fact her hair is no longer orange and there's a lot less of it. His using the name has her right back at school being teased mercilessly about what her mom called her 'crowning glory'. What had been meant as a term of endearment had been an unending taunt from the other kids. Halloween had been the worst.

Another wave of his hand and her dad has the dog back to his usual size.

Dex's body is consumed with a tsunami of shudders that wrack him from head to tail. *"That was awful. Never do that again. Like ever."* Rather than stay sitting on the log and risk getting caught up in another spell gone wrong, Dex jumps back onto Frankie's bed.

"Sorry, Dex." Colin strokes the small dog's wiry coat and tugs on his ears, affectionately. "I'm still a little shaky with these new powers of mine."

Perhaps it's all the years of practice he had before he was imprisoned? Either way, her dad has a better handle on his newly acquired powers than Frankie does on her own. Even so she finds it a teeny bit annoying. Whenever she tries a casual wave of her hand to reinforce a spell, it goes wrong. Nothing devastating so far, but give it time.

Zane, her merman boyfriend, has already hinted — make that nagged — that she needs to put in some practice, and soon. The way he tells it, without practice something is going to go spectacularly wrong. Say, like her manifesting a six foot long flaming yule log in the middle of her cabin, on a wooden boat. Yep, this counts.

Even with the length of wood a more manageable size and safely contained by a larger fireplace, Frankie is having second thoughts. The Wikipedia entry says she needs to keep it burning for the whole of the solstice celebrations. She happens to love her home and thoughts of it burning down to the waterline aren't going to have her sleeping easy. If at all.

Frankie grabs her wand, taking a moment to enjoy the connection this simple piece of wood has to her new powers. Perhaps she should have used it for the yule log? "Sorry, I'll have to come up with something else." A quick tap to the top of the fireplace and it disappears, along with the log. "It's just too risky."

"What about this?" Colin waves his hand at the large sideboard. Once the fog of unfamiliar magic clears, Frankie can see a beautifully set-up yule altar. It's similar to the one showing on the screen of her phone. And while there are naked flames in the form of candles, these are in beautifully painted glasses lessening the chances of accidental incineration.

That the altar must have some meaning to her dad is evident by the tears streaming down his face. His moving one of the candles a fraction to the left tells Frankie he's recreating something he's seen in the past. Any resemblance to the image on her phone must be purely coincidental.

"Your mom used to set it up like this every year."

Frankie's mouth drops open in surprise. "Not that I ever saw, she didn't."

"But..."

Frankie can see he's trying to remember back

to a time before his life was put on hold. His gaze darting backward and forward over the display in front of him tells her he's coming up empty. "But, but it was your mom's favorite holiday of the year. She always went all out for the coven."

"The coven? The Marina Coven is the first coven I've ever belonged to. It was just mom and me for years. And she hated the Winter Solstice with a passion."

This is an understatement. So averse was her mom to the celebration, Frankie was even barred from marking it on the calendar next to the phone in the kitchen. Anyone entering their home would have no clue there was an important event just around the corner.

She can see her dad is having trouble with the reality of her childhood. Obviously how he'd imagined it and her reality, being poles apart.

"I don't understand. Why would your mom stop living with a coven and celebrating the solstice? Unless..."

Frankie waits. And waits. It's getting to the point she thinks he's once again lost in his memories, when he breaks the silence.

"That must be it. I was taken on the first night of the solstice. With your mom needing to concentrate on your jinx, she must have felt it would be easier to distance herself from the coven."

Frankie and her dad are still staring at the yule altar when their thoughts are interrupted by a tinkling of bells. While familiar, it's not a sound Frankie's heard in a while. She wonders why Magda, an energy vamp with an aversion to blood, is back to announcing her arrival like this. The vampire then pops into focus.

A vampire popping up in her cabin doesn't alarm Frankie as it might some, with Magda preferring energy over blood. It's something more likely to have her snack saying, "I feel so tired," and not, "Wow, where's all my O-positive gone?"

That the normally gorgeous European has red-rimmed eyes is either down to allergies or a sign that she's been crying. Despite looks that could have her mistaken for a pageant princess, Magda is one of the toughest women Frankie knows. It's this that has her thinking Magda must be allergic to something, other than blood that is.

"I 'ave been called 'ome. I 'ave come to say goodbye." Magda sniffling into a pristine white handkerchief, reinforces she's not happy about it. Even the blonde locks that tumble the length of the woman's back are flat and dull.

"Do you have to go? We can all celebrate the solstice here."

"It is not for solstice I return. The sharing of blood is a tradition, I can avoid no longer."

"Sharing of blood? But I didn't think you, ah..." Frankie can't voice the rest of her question, allowing it to die on her lips. Like someone who's had all their blood sucked.

Magda blushes at Frankie's suggestion. "This, it is different. To share blood, ensure survival of my family."

Frankie's busting to pepper her friend with more questions; however, Magda holds her hand up stopping her from doing so. "I must leave."

Frankie isn't happy about her friend's departure, even though she knew this day would come. Magda is the first friend she's ever had where she can be herself, where she doesn't need to hide her magic or her borderline weirdness. Even as a kid, she lacked friends, making her closer to her mom than anyone else.

Frankie take's a deep breath before speaking; worried she'll break down if she hurries things. "When, when do you have to go?"

"Now." This simple response is followed by a sob from Magda that sucks half the energy out of the room and that sees Dex lying on his side, snoring gently.

"Oh, oh, I am so sorry." Magda places her hands gently on the Jack Russell's small body. Soon the familiar crackling starts up, and not long after Dex lifts his head. His eyes are wide and he's alert rather than drowsy.

"Why am I lying down? What just happened?"

"I am sorry, Mr Dex. I do not mean this." Magda runs her hand gently down his back, repeating the process until they're both calm.

Frankie yawns widely. "Any chance of a top-up, Magda?" While Frankie hasn't been knocked out like her familiar, her bed is looking mighty comfortable right now. Shame lying down isn't an option, with Colin prostrate next to Dex. His constant shaking of his head shows Magda has drawn a good deal of his energy too.

"I am so sorry. I do not mean to do this. It is always like this when I am upset."

No sooner has the vamp stopped speaking than Frankie is hit with a surge of energy that has her ready and raring to go. She's not sure where, but if she doesn't move soon, she's going to explode. Likewise her dad is upright again and positively bouncing on his feet.

"Probably didn't need quite this much," he

gasps out, before walking backward and forward in an effort to quell the buzz.

Magda's gaze swings from Colin to Frankie and back, with her wringing her hands together the whole time. "You are not safe around me. I 'ave to go home. To stay is dangerous for all."

In the knowledge her friend is likely to disappear any second, Frankie doesn't give herself time to think, she simply blurts it out. "What if we came with you?" On seeing the shocked look on Magda's face, she adds, "Just for the solstice."

Frankie knows her late mom would have a fit at her inviting herself to someone else's home like this. Tough, with her solstice planning being a bust, anything has to be better than spending the holiday here. She just hopes her dad is okay with it.

Magda goes from downcast to euphoric in a heartbeat letting Frankie know she's going to be spending the Winter Solstice in the Carpathian Mountains. That this will have her spending the holiday at vampire central clicks a second later, and she makes a mental note to pack plenty of turtleneck sweaters.

"Frankie if you could take Dex, we can be on our way." Magda then holds her hands wide in readiness to touch Colin and Frankie.

Frankie freezes right where she is, bent over ready to pick up her familiar. "But, we need to pack. We can't just up and leave. And what about Zane?"

"Yes, yes, but you must pack like the wind. Natalia does not wait for anyone. But know you this. Zane cannot come to my 'ome. The life energy would be sucked out of 'im and 'is body left out for the wolves. There 'as been bad blood for centuries."

"Centuries?" says Frankie. "Does anyone even remember what the original fight was about?" So often this is the case in these long-running feuds and she doubts this is any different. Surely the feud can't be bad enough to be life threatening for Zane?

Rather than answer, Magda shrugs leaving Frankie none the wiser. Her friend either knows and isn't saying anything, or doesn't have the first idea. "You pack quickly. I meet you at *The Crate* in 'alf an 'our and we travel to Castle Rhaetian."

Colin, apparently uninterested in the feud between the Zilonka family and the Nautilus people, blurts out, "Castle? You live in an actual castle?"

That his eyes are alight with excitement sits like lead in the bottom of Frankie's stomach. Never mind he's overlooked the whole *sucking the merman dry* reference. There's not a hope in Hades of her changing his mind about visiting Magda's home for the holidays. Thoughts of spending the solstice without Zane have Frankie swiping at her own eyes.

Unless that is, she's able to use her freaky new Wereall powers to mask him? Her own disguise had been undetectable by Magda; so perhaps she can do the same for her boyfriend. There's one way to find out, and for this she's going to need to be fast, and the disguise bullet-proof. Anything less and she'll be looking for a new boyfriend.

2

No sooner has Magda left for *The Crate,* the glorified shipping container Frankie once called home, than she turns to her dad. "Be back in a mo'. You'd better magic up a suitable wardrobe for yourself. It'll be cold."

Frankie pulls her wand out the back pocket of her jeans and waves it around her body, thinking of Zane and her need to be right next to him. It's the first time she's used this spell, so whether it will work is another thing.

Usually she'd simply zap herself over to his front door and knock like a *Normal.* However, if he's out, this will mean she's lost precious seconds, and it's time she doesn't have. The newly learned location spell is the fastest way for her to speak to him. No matter where he is.

He doesn't look overly happy to see her. Nor do the other men with him. Might be because the meeting she's crashed is being held in a sauna. It's a big one too. Big enough that it must be in a health club rather than a private home. Thank goodness for all those fluffy white towels.

For a moment Frankie forgets what it is she's here to talk to Zane about. It might be his muscled chest glistening with sweat, or the way the ends of his dark hair are curling riotously, softening him. Unable to help herself, Frankie drops her gaze. Now she isn't so much stunned as completely gob smacked. She'd thought he had to be in the sea for his merman tail to appear? A quick check shows a couple of the other mermen also have their tails on show.

She's still pondering where it is she's arrived, when Zane coughs to get her attention. There's nothing subtle about it.

Mesmerized by his deep blue eyes, it's a struggle to get the words out. "Oh, uh, right? I need to speak to you, urgently. Meet me back at your place."

Without giving him time to reply or even flex his pecs, Frankie transports herself to the back deck of his houseboat and waits. She's not had time to complete a return trip along the length of the deck when Zane pops into focus in front of her. She can't decide if she's disappointed or not that he's dressed.

"What was so urgent you had to find me no matter what state I was in?"

Frankie's unable to do anything about the rush of heat to her face on recalling exactly what that state had been, instead ignoring it in the interests of efficiency. The problem she's got is finding the right words to let Zane know what's happening, in the end settling for bullet points

"Magda's leaving. My place is never going to embrace the spirit of the Winter Solstice. I kinda invited myself, Dex and dad to spend the holiday with Magda. At her place."

It's when Frankie utters the last three words that Zane's countenance changes and he morphs from mildly annoyed to furious.

"You're actually going to travel to the other side of the world and spend the holidays with that pit of vipers?" While he might have started out quietly, the last few words are loud. Loud enough she takes a step back and comes close to falling off the side of the deck.

"But... but... I thought you liked Magda?"

"Magda I like. The other members of the Zilonka family, however, are evil personified. You can't go."

Frankie has to hold herself back from lecturing him on thinking he has any control over her decisions. Then she melts inside that he cares enough to get this riled. The strength of his reaction also has her wondering what the history is between the Nautilus and Rhaetian Clans. It seems odd peoples of the mountain and sea would come in close enough contact to even start a feud. Never mind one as bitter as this.

"If you're worried about my safety, you could always come with me."

"Right and die a slow and painful death. Not happening."

"What if you were in disguise?"

At Zane's bark of wry laughter, it dawns on Frankie he must be thinking of a standard glamor spell. Something that would be useless when dealing with energy vamps, or any kind of vamps, possibly.

Frankie holds her hand up to quell his laughter. "Before you say anything else, hear me out." Frankie, taking in the tic in Zane's left eye, doesn't wait for him to agree, or say anything else.

"I can mask you using my, ah, newer powers." Frankie doesn't mention the Wereall part of this equation, preferring to ignore the subject of her mixed heritage in hopes it'll go away. "It fooled Magda when I disguised myself and Dex for our first visit to the island. It should work on the other members of her family too. Heck, one of my disguises even fooled you and Stanley, our coven leader."

Zane opens his mouth. No words come out. Him clamping his lips together, turning on his heel and wandering off down the deck confirm he's at least thinking about it. However, he doesn't have long to decide, with the half hour Magda has given Frankie and her dad to pack, fast running out.

In the days before her jinx was lifted, Frankie would have had to race back to her place and throw clothes into a bag haphazardly. Instead a brief wave of her wand in the direction of the *Pearl* is all it takes. There's a Louis Vuitton carryall stuffed with warm comfortable clothing waiting for her in her cabin. Okay so what if the carryall is a knock-off, it's good enough to fool most people, and that's all that counts? Exactly like what she's got in mind for Zane.

She's magically adding a few last minute bits and pieces to her bag when Zane stops in front of her.

"What sort of disguise were you thinking of? Magda's going to know something's wonky if you turn up with some random stranger."

It's something Frankie already knows. It had been Dex retrieving a bag of his favorite biscuits so she wouldn't forget to pack them that gave her the idea. That Zane is asking tells of him coming around to her way of thinking. It looks as if they'll get to spend the holiday together after all, even if it's not as Frankie had hoped for. At this point, she'll take what she can get.

Frankie centers and calms her magical energy before looking him in the eye. "Do you trust me?"

His *yes* isn't as forceful as she'd like. Not that this stops her from acting on it, and she gives him a quick peck on the cheek by way of apology before pointing her wand at him.

Frankie doubts even Dex will be able to tell that the small pig standing in front of her isn't Spud. No-one else seeming to know which witch's familiar the small pig is and with the animal not seen for months; she knows this is the perfect disguise.

Zane's loud squeal of shock and horror is enough to have Frankie covering her ears. Unfortunately it does nothing to lessen the volume or his outrage. *"You have got to be kidding me. You turned me into a pig?"*

Frankie leans down and picks the small porker up. "Wow, I wasn't expecting the whole telepathic thing. I guess I really did channel Spud when I completed your disguise."

Frankie puts Zane down again although now they're back in her cabin on the *Pearl*.

Dex jumps down off the bed, his tail wagging delightedly. *"Spud, you came back."*

Frankie's pondering how to explain her subterfuge to her familiar when Zane beats her to it

"Yeah, yeah I did. Anything happen while I was away."

Better to let Dex think Spud really has returned than to risk someone overhearing his non-stop telepathic chatter. Who knew what the 'pit of vipers' were capable of. The following five minutes confirms for Frankie the decision to keep Dex in the dark has been the right one. Without pause he jabbers on, telling 'Spud' about EVERYTHING.

Zane's piggy mouth is soon hanging open. This

is less to do with the sheer volume of information and more to do with how much Dex is embellishing his stories. The way Dex tells it, he stormed *All Hallows Keep* on his own.

Even hearing the name of the place has Frankie taking hold of the amulet around her neck and running her thumb over the runes. The piece of jewelry is also the key that made it possible for her and the others to reach the keep, a prison for magical beings.

At least this is what it was supposed to be. The Garnets, the family that owns the island where the portal to *All Hallows Keep* is situated, had other ideas. Anyone stupid enough to cross them in business soon found themselves locked up.

Dex isn't close to running out of exploits when Colin walks back into the cabin. He's carrying a weekend bag and wearing what looks to be a new jacket and pants. His boots are similar in design to Frankie's own and will be perfect for tramping through snow, if the need arises.

"And who do we have here?" Colin crouches down and gently pats the small pig on the back of his head.

"This is, ah, Spud. He's coming with us rather than stay here on his own. Are you okay to say he's your familiar?"

Her dad gets back to his feet and spears Frankie with a look that has her squirming. "Frankie, you know how your mother felt about lying."

"It's only a little lie, and it doesn't seem fair that Spud should have to spend the holidays on his own just because we're leaving unexpectedly." Frankie crosses her fingers that this small serving of guilt will be enough to override Colin's aversion to telling porkies.

He looks from Frankie to the small pig and back again, his brow wrinkled in concentration. "Can't he spend the holiday with Zane?"

"Yeah," says Zane, "why can't I spend it with Zane." If Frankie wasn't looking at 'Spud' with her own eyes, she'd never have thought it was possible for a pig to smirk, but Zane's managing it.

Colin, however, isn't laughing. "Did that pig just speak?"

Ooops, this wasn't something Frankie envisaged. Usually it was only a familiar's witch who could hear them, or another familiar. Frankie is unusual in that she can communicate with all familiars in some form or another. It would appear this is a family trait. Unless it is that everyone can hear 'Spud'.

'Spud' ambles over and taps her dad's ankle

with a small trotter. *"If you can hear me, I must truly be your familiar."*

"There you go. You heard it yourself, straight from the pig's mouth. Let's go or we'll be late."

Despite not looking convinced, Colin leans over, picks up 'Spud', and then grabs his weekend bag. "Ready when you are."

Frankie likewise grabs Dex and her bag before shuffling over so she can make contact with her dad. The briefest wave of her wand sees them on the pier out front of *The Crate*.

They're in time to see Magda dragging her hot pink wheeled suitcase along the side dock. The merest flick of her eyes and she takes everyone in, although her gaze settles on 'Spud'. "And who is this?"

Dex, 'Spud' and Frankie all look at her, mute. It's her dad who answers.

"He's... he's my familiar. I'm hoping it's alright that I bring him along." As stilted as his delivery has been, Frankie doubts Magda is going to buy it. Here's hoping the language barrier will be enough for the lie to pass.

Magda drags her suitcase out onto the main dock, her expression one of skepticism. "Your familiar? I did not know you 'ad a familiar?"

"He... he arrived this, ah, morning. I don't know where from. But the connection is definitely there. I can hear his thoughts."

"In that case, 'e is very welcome to visit my family 'ome. We complete the circle, yes?"

With everyone and everything in the group touching in some way, Frankie waits for Magda to transport them to her home. Nothing happens and Frankie looks up from giving Dex another kiss on top of his head to find Magda looking at her expectantly.

"You want me to do it?" This gives Frankie a case of the jitters. She's got no problem ferrying everyone to and from the island. For her to take a group and their luggage to an unfamiliar location is a scary prospect. Even longitude and latitude would be a help. Her thoughts of the lost 'luggage' nightmare that could ensue must show, with Magda laughing delightedly.

"I give you the words. You say them and 'poof' we are 'ome."

"Okay. This I can do." Frankie frees her arm from Magda's and gets her wand out the side pocket of her bag. She then hooks her arm back through that of the energy vamp, making sure not to stab Magda in the process. While a little awkward, Frankie will still be able to swirl her wand enough to reinforce the spell. "Right, ready when you are."

Because of Magda's accent it takes every ounce of Frankie's concentration to ensure she says the words perfectly, adding any dropped Hs or missing words where necessary.

> *Bonny by blood and those of the heart,*
> *we call to our forebears as we depart.*
> *Take us to Rhaetian, safe true and strong,*
> *and welcome us there as if we belong.*
> *There we will stay as guest of the Crone*
> *and only the Maiden may send us back home.*
> *Thus we will soar, with limbs that are sound,*
> *until body and soul are once again bound.*

At the same time as uttering the last few words, Frankie executes a rather restricted wave of her wand. More than a little unnerved by the last couple of lines, she shuts her eyes and holds her breath. Just as well, as the whooshing and swirling that sees them leave Seattle for parts unknown, is enough to take anyone's breath away. Not to mention their stomach.

Only on feeling biting cold nibbling away at

her face does Frankie dare to open her eyes. The scene before her isn't what she's been expecting of Magda's home. It's anything but.

3

Other than the dwelling being far from castle-like, the most startling thing is the sheer volume of snow. The trees have lost their shape to it and the landscape is soft and fluffy with any rocks or structures piled high in white.

Magda unhooks her arm, freeing Frankie to stuff her wand up the sleeve of her puffer jacket. "Excellent, we 'ave arrived."

Colin, having dropped his bag in the snow next to him, spins himself and 'Spud' around. "And the castle? Where's the castle?"

Magda takes a step back. "I cannot simply arrive at the castle with surprise guests."

"Told you the place was dangerous," pipes up Zane, telepathically.

This has Magda's eyes widening and her spinning around as much as Frankie's dad just has. "Who... who said that?"

Bent broomsticks, this could be a problem. Frankie had thought only Colin, herself and Dex could hear Zane in his cover as Spud the runt pig. Looks as if she's wrong. Aware of her dad's inability to tell a believable lie, Frankie fills the gap with the first thing that comes to mind. "I didn't hear anything?"

Rather than respond, Colin examines the ground to avoid having to commit to another lie. Thank goodness Magda isn't able to hear Dex chattering away, or the pig would well and truly be out of the bag.

It's a long wait before the look of suspicion lifts from Magda's face. Only when she indulges in one of her all-purpose European shrugs, is Frankie able to relax. "You will spend the night 'ere and travel to my 'ome tomorrow."

Okay, so the cuckoo clock cottage they're standing out the front of is a halfway house of sorts. Frankie can live with this. The one thing she's not keen on is the set of footprints that start off in the middle of nowhere and lead to the front door of the cottage. It would appear whoever they belong to has transported in from somewhere else, as they have.

Magda draws in a lungful of frigid air, releasing it in a cloud of white. "First, we rid ourselves of whoever is inside. Yes?"

Frankie's eyes widen and she peers at the mullioned windows that pepper the front of the cottage before twisting her head to look to Magda. "You don't know who it is?"

"No. But if it is trolls, we will need to be vigilant." Magda drags her wheeled suitcase through the snow, in a beeline for the front door.

After picking up his bag, Colin follows with Spud, leaving Frankie and Dex to come up the rear.

"Dex, when you get ah, Spud alone can you tell him he's going to have to be quiet from here on in?" Frankie knows the merman has more than likely already worked this out and won't be happy about it. But, with everyone seemingly able to hear Zane's telepathic communications, the odds of discovery are no longer in their favor.

"Yep, sure can."

Magda isn't subtle about how she approaches the small house, instead striding through the snow as fast as her platform boots and wheeled suitcase will allow. She then swings the front door wide, demonstrating to Frankie it hasn't even been locked. Sure they're out in the middle of nowhere and so should be safe. But if trolls are as big a problem here as they are on social media, perhaps the Zilonkas should invest in some security.

Even though she's still a good distance from the cottage, Frankie's able to hear the familiar crackling. Magda busy siphoning energy from the dwelling, any living thing inside is either unconscious, or soon will be. However, the vamp doesn't enter just yet, instead beckoning to Frankie to join her.

Frankie trudges through the snow, still holding onto Dex. Much better this than putting him down and having the cottage smelling of wet dog. She joins the others on a front porch that's relatively free of snow, dropping her bag and stepping over to join Magda.

"I 'ave taken care of the vermin and... and something else. Perhaps you 'ad better be ready with your wand?"

"Something else?" Frankie stuffs her hand up the sleeve of her jacket, grabs her wand, and has it pointing inside the cottage soon after. "Dex, I'm going to put you down. No going inside, okay?"

"Sure Mom. I'll guard out here."

"Something else?" repeats Frankie, with Magda not having responded the first time.

"I am not sure. I am unable to remove the energy from the troll and this 'ad too much energy for the small pest."

Rather than lead the way as would be expected of the hostess, Magda shoves Frankie inside and trails after her. Frankie doesn't have a problem with this. Her new powers and Bruce Lee moves can take care of most eventualities, or even unwanted guests.

The only thing missing is Zane ready to fight at her side, with his masquerading as a small pig putting paid to this. Not that she needs his fighting skills. The biggest danger is hypothermia, with the inside of the cottage easily as cold as it is outside.

Frankie turns and makes eye contact with her dad. "The three of you had better stay there until we're sure the cottage is safe to enter." Not that he needs protection, with his powers probably equal to Frankie's own. It's more that Frankie needs him to keep an eye on the two animals. Even if one of them is a warlock/merman hybrid in disguise, Dex has delusions of grandeur when it comes to his strength, and they're in wolf territory. And then there are the trolls Magda has mentioned.

The cottage is small, with them able to see

straight away that the room they've entered is empty. There are two doors leading to other rooms and stairs to the second floor. Magda throws open the nearest door and Frankie storms in, her wand at the ready. It's almost a disappointment to find that what looks to be a laboratory is empty too.

They then cross to the other door and repeat the process. This time it's the kitchen, and it's occupied. It's who they discover there that has Frankie close to dropping her wand.

Frankie expected a troll like something from one of the books she read as a kid. Instead she's stunned to find her grandmamma lying on the kitchen floor. "Anne? What on earth are you doing here?" Anne snorts and settles into more regular snoring although how anyone can sleep on a tiled floor wearing a bikini is staggering. It's then Frankie remembers her grandmamma's unwanted donation of energy to Magda.

"I suppose we 'ad better get 'er up before she freezes."

Even though Magda's been the one to suggest it, she does nothing to hide her reluctance. It's something Frankie shares, not that she can follow through on it. Sure she's still annoyed with her grandmamma — doing a runner with the map and the treasure — but she's not going to let her die of cold, either. Even if she is horrible; she's also flesh and blood, family.

Frankie's surprised the spell Magda had given her has been so far reaching as to collect Anne from somewhere in the Caribbean. It must have been the words "Bonny by blood" that did it. That Anne was swimming rather than simply sunbathing at the time the spell took effect is shown by the fast-freezing puddle of water she's lying in.

Calico Jack must be freaking out about Anne suddenly vanishing. This is something that has Frankie indulging in a small smile. It's about time the wily pirate was as in the dark as Frankie is half the time.

The other thing her grandmamma's being here confirms for Frankie is that Anne, her dad, and herself are the only Bonnys left from their bloodline. Unless that is, they're incarcerated in *All Hallows Keep* thanks to Mimi the demon's crazy need for power? If they're in that hell hole, the most compelling spell known to witch-kind won't be strong enough to pull them free. Nope, the only way Frankie's can liberate her family, is with good old-fashioned martial arts and cunning.

Frankie leans over and puts her hand on her grandmamma's shoulder. "I'll take her back to the Caribbean. I shouldn't be long."

Magda holds her hand up to stall Frankie, all while shaking her head with a vehement 'NO!' "You will not be able to do that."

"I won't?" Frankie screws her face up, trying to remember if she's used any magic since she arrived. She comes up empty with there being no need to perform any. But surely she must be able to if Magda asked her to arm herself with her wand. Or was she just meant to use it to poke someone in the eye?

Magda continues to shake her head. "No, the spell is set. We must all remain until the Maiden has taken over from the Crone. To leave before is dangerous."

On hearing tiny trotters on tiles, Frankie turns to find 'Spud' right behind her. While Zane doesn't give voice to his thoughts, his little face is screwed up in a porky 'I told you so'.

Frankie turns back to Magda. "I can perform magic here, though, right?" Frankie knows to ask having learned the hard way never to take anything for granted. Perhaps it was all those years being jinxed and with her powers faltering just when she needed them that has her more cautious than most.

"Of course."

Frankie waits for the *but*, however there isn't

one. "Okay then, I'll chuck some suitable clothes on her and we can dump her on the couch with a blanket."

"You do not want me to return the energy to 'er?"

"Pilfering pirates no. Can you imagine the ear-bashing we'd get? Better to leave her to come around in her own time." Frankie would even be happy for her wayward grandmamma to sleep long enough that they can celebrate the solstice without her. There's nothing like the dead-weight of a cantankerous relative to ruin the holidays. Frankie also couldn't guarantee when it came time to leave that the booty-obsessed Anne wouldn't be weighed down with the Zilonka family silver.

A negligent wave of her wand and Frankie has her grandmamma dry and dressed from head-to-toe in thermal clothing. It's robust enough there won't be a chance of her freezing to death. That the whole ensemble is in a hideous pink is down to Frankie knowing her grandmamma will despise the color, preferring the autumnal tones that set off her red hair. These are colors Frankie favors too.

Magda then proves once again how strong she is by dragging Anne off the tiled floor and through to the main room. There she dumps the unconscious woman on the couch without ceremony before throwing a couple of animal skins over her in lieu of a blanket.

Meantime, Frankie has called out to the others that it's safe to enter. It's on doing so that she realizes Zane hadn't waited for the all-clear as she'd asked. It's this that has her lifting her eyebrow in his direction when he trots in from the kitchen.

Dex is the next of the group to see Anne, with his displeasure shown by a growl from the back of his throat and his hackles standing to attention. It isn't that the woman has ever harmed the small dog but more that he's intensely loyal to Frankie. If you've annoyed his mom, you've annoyed him. It's just as well Frankie's grandmamma isn't still lying on the ground because Dex would have 'marked' her by now.

Colin, however, is fascinated, standing next to the couch and staring down at Anne. "And who do we have here?"

Because Frankie and Anne bear a striking resemblance to each other, she knows her dad wants to hear how they're related more than anything else. Plonk a shoulder-length red wig on Frankie and she and Anne could easily be mistaken for twins. Never mind her grandmamma is well over three-hundred years old, although not all of these spent in the land of the living.

Frankie stands beside him and looks down at the woman sprawled on the couch. "This... this is the pirate Anne Bonny, your great, great, something grandmamma. Not sure how many greats there are in there."

"Anne? But she's long-dead."

"Not exactly," says Frankie, explaining to him how it is that their relative is back with them, even if she can't be classed as 'undead'. While Frankie has been known to call her grandmamma a few choice names, Zombie isn't one of them.

The same can't be said of Calico Jack, her great, great something or other grandpa, and partner to Anne in both life and 'death'. What he is, Frankie isn't entirely sure. All she knows is that magic — possibly of the dark variety — has something to do with him still being 'alive and kicking'. Although in his case it's more alive and nicking. Once a pirate, always a blinkin' pirate.

"But..." Colin looks at Frankie, his eyes full of pain. "If you've been able to resurrect Anne, why not your mother?"

4

Frankie knew this day would come. She just hadn't expected it to be so soon, or in such a location. Even having thought about it, she's no closer to knowing how she's going to break the news to her dad. Much as she'd love to, bringing her mom back to life isn't an option.

Aware of the difficult conversation Frankie and her dad are about to have, the others head upstairs. Now they're alone apart from Anne, whose snoring confirms they won't be overheard.

Frankie takes a couple of calming breaths. "It's like this. My bringing Anne back to life was a fluke. I think it was her wearing an amulet when she died that allowed the spell to work like it did." There's no need for Frankie to point out that her mom never wore an amulet. Colin knows this all too well with her mentioning the amulets having him fingering the one hanging around his own neck.

He's about to speak when Frankie puts her hand on his back. "The other ghosts didn't end up human." Frankie goes on to explain what happened to those who were caught up in her spell and his shoulders slump. Much as he wants his wife back, he wouldn't wish this on her.

There's also the small fact Frankie hasn't seen her mom as a ghost, with her only contact having been made through Magda and her crystal ball. There's been nothing since then, reinforcing her mom's assertion that she's happy where she is and that her life was one well lived, with no unfinished business. Would her mom change her tune if she knew her husband was alive and well? Perhaps she does know?

Magda, Dex and Zane arrive soon after the awkward exchange is over, indicating they've been standing at the top of the stairs waiting. It's something Frankie is grateful for, with this finishing the conversation between her and her dad more effectively than anything else. She can see he's still thinking about possible solutions by the way he keeps opening and closing his mouth as if to give voice to them. She'd rather avoid upsetting him more than she already has, by continuing to say 'no'.

Frankie leaves him looking down at the un-conscious Anne and joins the others at the bottom of the stairs. "Did you find anyone or anything else?"

Dex stops scratching his side with his back leg long enough to reply. *"All clear. Although I think this place has fleas."*

"No we 'ave taken care of all the other vermin," says Magda, looking pointedly at the couch.

Rather than respond telepathically and give the game away, Zane shakes his head.

"Good, let us make ourselves at 'ome." Magda drags her suitcase inside, parks it next to Frankie and her dad's bags and then shuts the front door. The room doesn't feel any cozier for it although this all changes when Magda claps her hands dra-matically above her head.

The wood sitting in the large fireplace ignites as though doused with petrol and candles flare into life around the room. It's like one of those lights you turn on by clapping your hands, on steroids. Frankie sniffs the air. Surely it's her imag-ination? She sniffs again. Nope, it's for real. She hurries through to the kitchen, her mouth already watering in response to the delicious smells emanating from there.

Sure enough on entering the previously frigid room, Frankie's met with steam coming out of pots on top of the stove. They definitely hadn't been their earlier. Nor had the room been this warm which she puts down to the heat rolling off the stove in waves. Frankie grabs a cloth and opens the door expectantly. "Wow that looks good." Here's hoping Zane in his current form as 'Spud' isn't to upset by them all chowing down on roast pork for dinner.

Frankie closes the stove door and tosses the cloth back on the counter and returns to the lounge. "Magda, I didn't realize you could perform magic."

"It is not me, it is the cottage. It has been spelled by many powerful family friends."

Frankie's trying to work out how this would be possible and how handy it would be to come home to a meal already underway, when Magda interrupts her thoughts.

"I will leave you now. I must speak to Natalia and get permission for ah... yes I must speak to Natalia."

The worry on Magda's face soon spikes Frankie's own. "Are you sure it's okay us being here?" Despite her having invited them all along in an effort to give her dad a solstice to remember, there are limits. There's the blood sharing tradition for a start.

"It is not this. It is something else, something I 'ave avoided as long as I could."

"What? What is it? You can tell me."

Magda doesn't take Frankie up on her offer to share. Instead, after the briefest of tinkling bells, the four of them find themselves on their own. Well, the five if you count Anne. Although with her grandmamma out for the count, mayhap you can't. Count her that is. Frankie gives up trying to decide.

Not that her mind is quiet, with her wondering what it is Magda has been avoiding. One thing there's no avoiding is the smell of roast pork wafting in from the kitchen. "Who's hungry?"

There's a cry of *yes* from everyone, except Anne.

Despite them taking their time over dinner, and even enjoying a round of hot chocolate and marshmallows after, there's still no sign of Magda. They're losing a fight with sleep before reluctantly turning in for the night. They leave Anne snoring loudly to go in search of suitable bedrooms. Frankie and Dex share a room as they always do. Zane and Colin, however, don't feel the need to take their charade of warlock and familiar to this degree. Instead they opt for separate bedrooms, leaving one room free for Magda if she returns before daybreak.

She doesn't.

It's late the next day before their hostess returns. That she's looking both saddened and nervous has Frankie more on edge than the extended wait has her. She leans forward in her seat next to the fire. "What's wrong?"

"I 'ad 'oped it would not 'appen." Magda takes a couple of shuddering breaths, trying to get herself under control. She's no calmer when she continues. "The blood price, it 'as been paid."

Frankie's no clearer on what it is that's upset her friend, and is ready with a volley of questions, when she's stopped. The cough, while telepathic, has been forceful, causing Frankie to look to Zane. That he's shaking his little piggy head slowly from side to side says it all.

Because the cough could have come from anyone, no-one questions it. Instead the group looks to Magda, waiting for her to elaborate. Not that she gives much away. "Ah, ah, it is nothing. It will be fine. We stick together." Her pointy teeth on show, Magda's smile fails to reassure Frankie in the least.

"Look, if it's a problem, we can stay here." While it isn't Frankie's first choice, if their visit to the castle is going to result in a family argument, or death, she'd rather avoid it. Colin's mouth turning down at the sides indicates he's not happy with her suggestion.

"Awww Mom, I wanted to see a real live castle."

The one member of the group who looks pleased to be staying put is Zane. He makes quite the show of flopping down on the bear skin rug in front of the fire. Frankie worries if he gets any closer he's going to risk losing a bristle or two. The still unconscious Anne doesn't seem to care either way.

Frankie succumbs to the silent pleas of Dex and her dad, and struggles to her feet, ignoring Zane's wishes. "Fine, I'll go grab my bag from my bedroom."

Colin hauls himself out of the large armchair he's claimed as his own and is halfway up the stairs before Frankie's even taken two steps. She's not even made it to her room, when she hears the clatter of tiny trotters on the wooden stairs.

"Are you out of your mind?"

Frankie puts her finger to her lips, not sure how far his telepathic rant will travel. This is one conversation, she doesn't want Magda, or any Zilonka, overhearing.

Zane continues, his voice so low inside her head, that even she's having trouble hearing what he's saying. This should be okay.

"If the family doesn't want us there, it's not going to be pleasant. From what my family says, the Zilonkas can be a nasty bunch at the best of times."

"But I can't disappoint my dad. It'll be his first solstice in over twenty years. You saw his face. Dex is busting to see a real castle too."

"I don't like this. It would be one thing if we were welcome, but this..."

"We'll just need to be on our guard," whispers Frankie, in response. "But never mind that, what's all this about a blood price?"

Zane stills, as if searching for the right words. *"I've heard of it, but I thought it died out in the 1970s."*

"And..."

"It's an arranged marriage with someone from another vampire family to keep the blood lines pure.

That's why it's called a blood price. It's what you and I would call a dowry."

"An arranged marriage, but that's archaic. No wonder Magda's down in the dumps about it. We have to stop it."

"I keep forgetting you were brought up amongst Normals. There's nothing we can do about it. And nothing we're going to do about it. With the blood price paid, the marriage is already set in stone. The one thing that can stop it is the death of either the bride or groom."

Frankie stalks backward and forward next to the old-fashioned oak bed before coming to a sudden stop. "If needs must!"

"Frankie! You are not to get involved. To meddle could lead to death, and I'm not talking about the groom."

"I'll put heavy duty wards around all of us before we leave. I can get my dad to help."

"What do you want my help with?"

Frankie spins in alarm. She's been so busy thinking up ways of getting rid of an unwanted groom, that she hadn't seen him standing in the doorway of her room. She's going to have to be on her guard better than this if the Zilonkas are as rabid as Zane makes out.

"Um, ah, 'Spud' is saying the Zilonkas are, ah."

Frankie runs out of words, unsure of how to describe their host family with her only having met Magda. Her friend is great. The rest of the family must be awful if they're paying for someone to take Magda off their hands.

Colin takes a step in Frankie's direction. "Are what?"

She doesn't need to find the right words, with Zane not holding back in his whispered summary of what the Zilonkas are famous for. Or in this case infamous. Wow, Magda really is the black sheep of the family. Make that the white sheep. No wonder Zane hadn't wanted Frankie to go in the first place and is trying to hold back on them visiting the actual castle.

Colin's eyes are as wide as Frankie suspects hers are.

He slings his bag onto Frankie's bed and grabs his wand out one of the zippered side pockets. "Double wards it is then. Frankie, get your wand."

"Hang on. I'll call Dex. He'll need protection too."

After Frankie puts out a telepathic 'here boy' the group waits, with the clatter of toenails on oak floorboards letting them know he's on his way. He spins into the room soon after. *What's happening?*

"We need to put a ward on all of us. Just in case

we run into any, ah, trolls." Much as Frankie would like to tell Dex about the potential dangers, she knows this will have him anxious enough that Magda will know something's up.

Only once the four of them are warded up the wazoo, do they make their way back downstairs in readiness to travel to Castle Rhaetian.

Frankie's surprised to see Magda swipe at her eyes with the back of her hand before turning away from them to stare into the fire.

Frankie holds her hand up to stop the others from following and walks over to stand next to her friend. She gently puts her arm around Magda's shoulders and is immediately glad she's sporting a bullet-proof ward. Without it, she'd be flat out on the floor having forgotten how her friend sucked energy when she was upset.

"Listen, if your family doesn't want us visiting, we can't barge in there like this."

As much as Frankie wants to talk to Magda about the arranged marriage, she holds back. Better to talk about subjects she's supposed to know about.

"It is not that they do not want you. It is perhaps that they want you too much."

It takes longer than it should for Frankie to decipher this. "Oh. Oh, right? Will we be okay?"

"I will protect you, with my life!" Magda drags Frankie into an embrace and squeezes her hard enough that a squeak pops out. "Ooooh, I am sorry." Magda releases her so abruptly, Frankie has to take a step back to keep her balance.

"And who exactly will you be protecting us from?" One thing all the years of martial arts training has taught Frankie is that it pays to know your enemy. Is Magda talking one or two family members, or all of them? One or two she can handle, but a whole clan of vampires? Now that's a challenge she'd rather avoid.

"It is Natalia. She is, how you say, our matriarch."

Okay, one little old lady, I can deal with that. Only on seeing the small piggy charade going on behind Magda does Frankie twig Zane has worked out what she's thinking. His falling over, and lying on his back with his little trotters in the air, tells her Natalia is dangerous, perhaps even lethal. Funny, he hadn't mentioned anything about her upstairs.

Frankie thinks about it briefly. Her friend needs to know and it might even mean they're safer too. "Magda, before we head to the castle, there's something I need to tell you." An abrupt *rat-ta-tat* of a small trotter on a floorboard tells Frankie that Zane isn't in agreement with her plan.

Tough, Frankie's gut is telling her they need to have her dad and Magda in on this particular secret. It's the only way they can be sure Zane will get through the holiday without ending up as the star attraction at the banquet. And not in a good way.

5

Magda looks at Zane in his disguise as Spud, shaking her head in disbelief. "I cannot sense anything, just as when you hid yourself."

Frankie's dad completes yet another circuit of the small pig. "It's as if he really is a pig." Of course this is after the dressing down he's already given Frankie for lying to him about who Spud actually is. If it wasn't for Frankie being twenty-five and them away from home, she suspects she'd be grounded by now. "But how is this even possible?"

Frankie shrugs a la Magda liking the ambiguity it provides. "I used my Wereall powers to complete the transformation, rather than my witchy ones."

Her dad leans over and strokes one of Zane's

ears. "They are the masters of the masquerade. It is perhaps too good."

Frankie's brow wrinkles in confusion. "Too good?"

Magda moves over to stand next to Frankie's dad, the pair of them staring at Zane.

"If I cannot sense 'e is not a pig, 'ow will my family know?"

Frankie tilts her head to the side. "Isn't that the whole point?"

"I think what Magda means is that if the family thinks I really am a pig, I could well end up on the menu. Am I right?"

Magda nods, confirming he's on the money.

"Well, I'll just change him into something else."

Frankie has her wand in her hand and is ready to go, when Magda shouts, "No!'"

Turns out even though Frankie's able to perform witch magic in the grounds of Castle Rhaetian, this is it on the magic front. To perform a spell, using her newly acquired Wereall powers would be to have castle guards descending en masse. It would have been good if Magda had explained this earlier, like before they left Seattle.

Frankie drops into what she thinks of as her chair, leans back and closes her eyes. There must be something she can do to avoid Zane ending up as part of the main course at the solstice banquet. Sensing someone is about to speak, she holds up her hand. Now the only sounds in the room are of Zane clattering about and Anne snoring.

Then it comes to her. "I've got it. We just used our witchy powers to throw up the wards, right?"

She gets nods all round.

"No castle guards, right?"

Again she gets a round of nods.

"What if I tweak the disguise so it's obvious he's, ah, a familiar? That would work, wouldn't it?"

Dex walking out of the kitchen licking his lips has Frankie putting a finger to her own. They need to be careful, with the small dog able to eavesdrop with the best of them. And, while she's happy for her dad and Magda to be in on the deception, Dex is a different story. His tendency to chatter telepathically could result in their ruse being blown dramatically. Who knew who, or what, could hear the Jack Russell other than Zane and her?

Magda stares into the fire longer than Frankie would like before turning to face her. That her friend is beaming answers Frankie's question about whether it's okay to use her witchy powers. Magda's smile then falters. "But 'ow?"

Dex looks at Magda, then everyone else. *"How what?"* He really does like to know what's going on.

Frankie doesn't bother answering either Magda or Dex, instead pointing her wand at Zane and muttering an incantation under her breath. Soon after this the room erupts in laughter, with none of it Zane's.

He twists his head first to one side, and then the other. *"This, this is the best you could come up with?"*

Frankie's unable to stop her giggles, instead talking through them. "I think they look cute."

Dex, who's been standing next to Zane during the transformation, sniffs the wings tentatively, before turning to Frankie. *"Cool! I want a pair too. I'd be a Flap Jack Russell! Please, Mom. Please."*

"Sorry, granola boy, no can do. You get into enough trouble on the ground."

Zane doesn't share Dex's enthusiasm for the new addition. *"They're not even big enough to get me off the ground if I'm in danger."*

He's got a point, and it's something that's rectified with the next wave of Frankie's wand. "Give them a go. See if they work."

Zane flaps his newly acquired wings and gets himself a foot off the ground before taking out a vase and a small figurine. This has him settling back down and retracting his wings so they sit tight against his back.

"Perhaps I'd better go outside?"

Magda, who's looking through one of the skinny windows next to the front door doesn't think this is a good idea. "We 'ave company and they look 'ungry. We leave now. She grabs the handle of her suitcase and drags it over next to the couch. "Quick, we must go before it is too late."

Curiosity getting the better of her, Frankie looks out the nearest window. What she sees is enough to have her racing to grab her and her dad's bags from the bottom of the stairs. She's soon next to Magda with Colin following suit. A click of her fingers and Dex is hard up against her left leg, with Zane against her right.

All of them touching, in some shape or form, Magda again claps her hands above her head. The fire and candles die immediately and Frankie suspects the kitchen will once again be spotless. She wants this spell for the *Pearl*. She's making a mental note to ask Magda about it when the front door crashes open.

Frankie has to blink twice to make sure her eyes aren't having her on. Unfortunately they're not. Magda's right, they do look 'ungry, not to mention ferocious and a more than a little on the wild side. Frankie's therefore pleased when Magda claps her hands together again not giving the new arrivals time to introduce themselves.

Before you can say medieval fortress, the six of them are in the entrance hall at Castle Rhaetian. The place is breathtaking if you're a fan of the Bram Stoker School of interior design. Creepy doesn't begin to describe it.

Even weirder than the décor is finding they're alone in the huge space. Frankie would have expected at least one or two people to be about. Surely you'd need servants to run a place the size of the castle? If nothing else, Frankie somehow expected Magda's fiancé would be here to greet her.

Perhaps this is why Magda is looking around as much as Frankie, Colin and the other two. "I 'ad 'oped to 'ave more time to prepare you."

"Like what?" says Frankie, checking out the imposing staircase that clings to the walls of the square hall for at least five stories.

"It is Natalia. She is 'ead of my family. She is old and cranky. Speak when spoken to. Laugh at ALL her jokes. Do NOT make eye contact."

No sooner has Magda finished her list of *do or dies* than Frankie spots a woman walking down the stairs. She's taking her time, giving the group plenty of opportunity to check her out. Frankie doubts it's the dreaded Natalia as the woman looks to be about the same age as Magda and herself. The new arrival might even be younger than twenty-five.

Her dark hair is tightly braided and sits atop her head like a crown while ribbons of pure power swirl around her in a veil. The design of her dress however appears older than dirt and is a good match to the castle itself. Dark burgundy velvet, the dress is fitted from neck to hip before flaring gently. Likewise the sleeves are tight down to the elbow before widening.

Devoid of jewelry her outfit would be plain but for the wide belt of gold that sits low on the woman's hips. Frankie puts it conservatively as being worth more than the *Pearl* AND Zane's houseboat combined.

It's not until she glides down the final flight to join them that Frankie can see there's nothing young about the woman's eyes. It isn't that she's got wrinkles; it's more that they contain the wisdom of the ages, along with a healthy dose of pure unadulterated evil. It's the sort of malevolence that takes centuries to accumulate.

Only then does Frankie remember the final item on Magda's list and drop her gaze to stare at the floor. While not usually submissive, Frankie knows meek and mild is the right approach when meeting a creature like this for the first time. She's one terrifying lady. Frankie scoots her gaze to the side and is able to see everyone else has assumed a similar posture, even Zane and Dex.

No one says a word to the point you could cut the tension in the air with one of the huge battleaxes hanging above a nearby set of double doors.

"So these are the guests you 'ave decided we should entertain." That she makes no mention of the fact the guests are three redheads, a Jack Russell, and a pig strikes Frankie as weird as all get out. That one of the red heads is out cold on the floor, surely rates a passing comment, but nope. "And you 'ave brought something for the banquet."

Zane catches on quicker than Frankie, and spreads his wings, demonstrating there's nothing 'main course' about him. Natalia's disappointment is a palpable thing. The big sigh Frankie hears inside her head, lets her know Zane's relief at being off the menu is just as heartfelt.

At such a lackluster welcome, Frankie envies her unconscious grandmamma and would happily swap spots. Even better, she'd like to be back on the *Pearl* and never mind that her cabin is thin on appropriate decorations. For sure she doesn't have room for a fir tree the size of the one tucked in a corner of the enormous entrance way. The beast has to be forty feet if it's an inch and sporting enough lights it could be seen from space.

It must be a nightmare keeping on top of all the dropped needles that are part and parcel of having a live tree inside the house. Or in this case castle. Not that there are any on the polished wooden floor under the tree. However a quick peek under the bottom branches shows there's a large wooden tub. Wow, the tree is alive, rather than waiting to turn into something that will be hidden behind the garage until it's a skeleton of its former self.

Perhaps the most striking thing about the tree is the silver mermaid that sits atop it in place of the usual fairy. On hearing a little piggy gasp from around her ankles, Frankie looks at Zane and can see his eyes are locked on the top of the tree. Could this be what the feud is all about? Certainly it's odd for a family who lives in the middle of a mountainous region to have a symbol of the sea adorning their solstice fir.

Magda coughs and Frankie turns away from the fir to look at her friend as no doubt intended.

"Yes Natalia, their 'all is barren. They 'ave need of your traditions. They are lacking."

On catching a glimpse of her dad lifting his head out the corner of her eye, Frankie grabs his wrist in a death grip. She's relieved to see his chin drop back down. The last thing they need is him waxing lyrical about the traditions of his family. Frankie's happy to let Magda take the lead on these negotiations. Because there's no doubt this is what they are. Okay and there's also a lot of ego-stroking going on, with the whole *your traditions* and *lacking* and such like.

Being stuck here until the solstice celebrations are completed, it's either stay in the castle or head back to the halfway house. To share a place that small with the trolls who'd arrived just as they were leaving would not be a fun time. At least Frankie thinks they were trolls.

They weren't quite as ugly as the illustrations in the books her mom had given her to read when she was little. A bit of a makeover the three of them could even pass for cute in a Jason Momoa kinda way.

It's Natalia speaking again that has Frankie's mind back on their current predicament.

"Fine if they 'ave need of proper tradition, they are *welcome* to stay."

It's hardly reassuring that the word 'welcome' catches on Natalia's tongue. However, with the group not in a position to be picky, they need to live with it.

Magda's sigh of relief bounces around the hallway, and Frankie's aware her dad's breathing has evened out too. She, however, doesn't share their optimism.

"But," says Natalia, causing hitches in both Magda and Colin's breathing.

Now, why did Frankie know this was coming? Perhaps because it always did?

"Your young friends will be confined to their rooms for this evening's festivities. Following this they will be free to move about."

Again Frankie has to grab her dad's wrist. Jinxed jellyfish, she knows he's keen to enjoy the solstice celebrations, but you do not argue with a matriarch as malevolent as this.

It doesn't matter how gorgeous Natalia might appear on the outside, she's powerful and potentially dangerous. As with Magda, Natalia is at the top end of the beauty queen scale. However, where Magda is blonde and a beacon of light, Natalia is dark, no doubt with a soul to match. If she hasn't sold it already.

There's nothing light about Magda at this moment, with her head bowed and her shoulders hunched as she tries to appear as small as possible. Frankie hates seeing her friend like this, but isn't about to voice her objections, right now.

"It will be as you wish, *Baba*."

Only after Natalia has left the hallway through large double doors, does Magda lead the group up the stairs to the very top of the castle. That she does this with an unconscious Anne slung over one shoulder impresses the heck out of Frankie.

His little piggy legs being as short as they are, Zane decides flying is an easier option. It's also the perfect opportunity for him to test his wings in a space where he won't take out any ornaments. He does, however, fly dangerously close to the mermaid atop the tree on his way to what must be the castle's attics. Any higher and they'd be hanging out with the resident bats.

Magda walks into the first room they come to and slings Anne onto the simple bed in there, leaving her to fall as she may. She then shuts the door on Frankie's grandmamma and moves along to the next doorway. "Frankie, Dex, this is your room. Colin, you and Z... Spud, are in the room opposite."

Dex wastes no time in trotting into his and Frankie's room, ready to sniff anything within reach. Likewise Zane and Colin soon disappear through the door of their allotted room.

"Magda, thank you for having us to stay. If we'd realized it was going to be so difficult for you, we'd never have come."

"I am glad you are 'ere. The traditions will be easier to bear now. At least I 'ope this is so."

"Yeah, speaking of traditions, what's with us having to stay up here tonight?" Sure Frankie's being nosy, she's also happier when she knows what's going on. It's saved her from being hurt in the past, making it a habit now.

Turns out it's for their own safety with the first night of the solstice being for the family. This involves some sort of ritual in which the whole clan share energy, and for an outsider to stumble into this would be to ensure instant death.

"Instant death?"

"Yes. Promise me Frankie, you must stay up here tonight. I will 'ave meals sent up and there is a big screen television in the room down the 'all. We are not as primitive as our 'ome would suggest."

Despite her promise to herself, Frankie can keep quiet no longer. "Are you sure there isn't any way to stop your engagement?" Frankie isn't sure if 'engagement' is the right term when you've been sold to the highest bidder. Auction feels more appropriate.

That Frankie knows of her engagement obviously comes as a surprise, with Magda's mouth forming a perfect O before she responds. "'ow do you know of this?"

"Zane's heard of it before. Is there nothing you can do to get out of it?"

"No! The blood price it 'as been paid. I will meet the man Natalia has chosen for me when we join 'ands in the family crypt."

Surely Frankie didn't hear that right? "Crypt?"

"Yes it is tradition that the forebears witness the sharing of the first blood."

What sort of guy allows himself to be hitched to a woman he's never met? Frankie doesn't like any of the images that spring to mind, with each bringing a bigger shudder than the last. Old and ugly is seemingly the common thread.

She's close to tears when she hugs her friend before Magda walks back down the stairs. It's as though her friend is dying rather than simply getting hitched. She can't imagine how dreadful it must be to know you're committed to marrying someone sight unseen, especially with that repugnant woman in charge of the selection process.

Magda hasn't gone far down the stairs when she stops. "I will come and get you in the morning. Do not go anywhere without me by your side. Stay safe."

Frankie walks over to the top of the stairs and watches her friend's progress right until she reaches the first floor. On spotting the three beings that'd slammed into the cottage earlier crossing the hall at speed, Frankie gasps. She's about to transport herself down there and kick some troll bahooty, when the three enfold Magda in a hug that has the vamp laughing with delight.

Frankie's enjoying watching her friend smiling for a change when one of the males looks up. She yanks herself back, unsure if she's done so in time. Slowly, she backs away from the balustrade until she's safely through the doorway of her and Dex's bedroom. She closes the door and slams home the three industrial strength bolts spaced out down length of the door. This more than anything shows her what a fortress her bedroom is designed to be.

Frankie leans against the door while watching Dex disappear under the large four-poster that dominates the room. She waits. Sure enough she becomes aware of breathing on the other side of the slab of wood. If she wasn't standing with her ear jammed hard against the door, she'd never have heard the words whispered to her. "Ta ha zemrën!"

Unfamiliar with the local language, Frankie doesn't have a clue what it means, she's hoping *Google* translate will. If she can spell it correctly that is. One thing that's not lost in translation is the guy's husky voice, with it playing her nerve endings like a virtuoso.

6

On hearing another knock on her door Frankie looks up from the note she's been tapping into her phone. If it's her very own troll back for another go at storming her defenses, she's going to let him feel the sharp end of her wand. It's almost a letdown when her dad calls out that their food has arrived.

Thoughts of something like last night's roast pork have Frankie drooling in anticipation and hurrying to join the others. Dex doesn't need to be asked twice to follow. Unfortunately, the food tonight is utilitarian and over-cooked to the point any crispness or color is long gone. It's the first time Frankie's ever eaten a grey potato. If they'd known this was what was on offer, they'd have brought leftovers from the cottage.

The rest of their evening is also lacking in color. While the television in the room at the end of the hall is one of the biggest Frankie's ever seen, the movie selection is the smallest. No cable for the Zilonkas by the looks of things.

Her dad isn't happy they're stuck up here while there's a party going on downstairs, not letting up on voicing his displeasure. This is until Frankie tells him to stop his whinging. She didn't risk her life saving him, for him to turn around and get himself killed.

"I'm sorry, *Pumpkin*. It's just that after so many years locked up, I want to live."

"I know dad, but going downstairs tonight will have you sucked drier than a wedge of lemon at a tequila bar."

The evening's a bust. Everyone makes excuses to go to bed to get away from the bad energy the argument has created. Frankie is the last to retire, turning off the television and the lights. It isn't how she wanted the night to end, but her dad needed the reality check, in a big way.

Frankie hasn't even had time to undress for bed when there's a light tap on her bedroom door. "Not again!"

While there aren't endless possibilities as to who it could be, there's one way to be sure. And if it is who she thinks it is, she's going to enjoy sending him downstairs with a flea in his ear. Frankie picks her wand up from the bedside table and pads over to the securely locked door.

"Frankie, open up. Quick."

Even though the words have been whispered through the solid door, Frankie knows exactly who her late night visitor is. Not any of those she's been expecting for sure.

Sliding the three bolts to the side, she opens the door and Magda skips into her room. Frankie's just as quick to slide the bolts back again, taking her cue from Magda who has a serious case of the jitters.

"What is it? Is your betrothed here?" It's the one thing Frankie can think of that would have Magda so keen to hide.

Magda goes from nervous to being shocked. "No! It is forbidden that I see 'im before the ceremony."

There's no doubt in Frankie's mind as to why this is. Not good for the blushing bride to see the ugly old dude before the ceremony. There's a greater chance of her doing a runner this way.

Frankie waits. Magda's obviously snuck up here for a reason.

"I want to... I..."

"Yes?" Frankie sits in one of the chairs next to the mullioned window that takes up most of one wall. This looks like it could take a while.

Magda takes a cue from Frankie sitting down, to get on with her story. She stumbles over her words in an attempt to get them out in a way Frankie can understand.

"I want to visit the local tavern one more time. When I am married woman, this will be forbidden."

"Forbidden?" What is it with the Zilonkas living in the dark ages? No wonder Magda had escaped to Seattle. Frankie had thought her friend staying in *The Crate* while on holiday was odd. Now she knows what the woman was avoiding, she understands.

"O.M.G, this will be like your bachelorette party!" Frankie jumps to her feet ready to make this the best bachelorette party ever. Frankie's never had a close friend, let alone one about to tie the knot. She's going to make a better go of this than her solstice celebrations.

There's one thing wrong. Magda doesn't look to be as enthused about having a party. Eventually she holds her hand up, stopping Frankie in her manic list making. "We cannot do that."

"Can't do what?" Frankie rattles off the last few items on her virtual list. "The veil, the exploding wedding cake, or us dancing on the bar?"

"None of them. If Natalia found out I'd snuck away from the celebrations, I'd be punished. Severely."

"What if no one knew who you were?"

"But, I do not understand. Everyone at the *Maramarosh Tavern* will know me."

"Not after I've finished, they won't. Do you trust me?"

Magda does, although she has second thoughts when looking at her image in the mirror. "But I can't go out looking like Natalia. What if she finds out?"

"I don't see how she can, she's busy isn't she? And anyway I haven't given you her energy, just her girlish good looks. Come on, time's a wasting. Now where is this place?"

Luckily it's close enough that Magda can actually point out the lights through the window of Frankie's room. A swirl of her wand and Frankie has the pair of them standing at the front door of the local hostelry. Now that she's made the commitment, Magda is all for it. She pushes open the door allowing light and noise to spill out onto the quiet country road.

On entering the tavern, Frankie's delighted to find it's exactly as she hoped it would be. There's a barrel ceiling, a surfeit of dark oak furniture and walls covered in Romanian knickknacks. While not exactly the nightclub most brides would choose for their bachelorette party, it's as good as it gets this close to the castle.

Frankie not having any of the local currency, it's up to Magda to get their drinks. There being few other patrons, it's not long before her friend puts two stone tankards on the table Frankie has nabbed.

Frankie takes another sip. "Wow, this stuff is strong." As with her first sip, she blows out to quell the burning in her mouth. She's going to have to pace herself or she really will end up dancing on the bar, something she'd been joking about earlier.

Frankie puts her tankard down and pulls her phone from the pocket of her hoodie. Surely she'll have more luck with Magda than she had with *Google* earlier in the evening? Reading out the words she'd typed in phonetically brings about a far better result. Not that it's one she's happy with.

Frankie stares aghast at Magda. "It means what?"

Instead of looking worried, her friend smiles broadly, something that's completely out of place on Natalia's face. "It means 'I'll eat your heart', but it is not threat. It is term of, 'ow you say, endearment."

"Strange way to tell someone you care," mutters Frankie.

They haven't even made it half way through their tankards of the local brew, when two men, who don't look to be locals, join them at their table. Both men are gorgeous. Not that Frankie is on the lookout for anyone, being more than happy with Zane.

The guy who sits next to Magda looks stunned and Frankie's got a good idea why. Here's hoping Magda is up to pulling off the charade to avoid them being caught out.

However, it's the guy sitting next to Frankie who grills Magda in the local dialect. Even unable to understand the words themselves, Frankie knows an interrogation when she hears one. She's left at a disadvantage until Magda, fully channeling Natalia, asks him to speak English as a courtesy to her guest.

Unfortunately this has him turning to look at Frankie and it's not a pleasant experience, despite his good looks. The guy has laser vision of the sort that would have you admitting to anything, whether you're guilty, or not.

"You are English?"

The dead look in his eyes and the timbre of his voice do strange things to Frankie. Strange, as in cockroaches crawling all over you, strange. There's nothing she can do about the full-body shudder this invokes. *Creeeeeepy!*

Unable to speak while being seriously grossed out, she nods her response. It's much easier for her to fake being English than actually have to talk to the guy. Not that she thinks she could speak to him, anyway. He's seriously disturbing.

Seemingly happy with her response, he returns his hypnotic gaze on Magda. "Natalia, this is the last place I would expect to see you."

Magda shrugs rather than commit herself fully to her assigned role. Could it be she finds it impossible to speak to creepy man too? Or could it be that she's so transfixed by the guy sitting next to her that she's incapable of rational thought? The sparks jumping between the pair of them point to it being the latter.

The two on the other side of the table having eyes for no one but each other, Frankie's stuck with the cockroach wrangler. Unable and unwilling to speak to him, Frankie stares at her drink, hoping he'll get the message and leave. No such luck. Nor does he stay silent, introducing himself as Dracul, a name so ludicrously close to Dracula that Frankie has to bite her lip to spot herself from laughing. The jumped up twit really is full of himself with every word out of his mouth designed to stroke his own ego. Seriously?

Frankie puts her hand over her mouth to smother yet another yawn. She'd think she was having her energy siphoned if not for the killer ward she and her dad had completed earlier that day. Nope, this is more to do with it being close to four in the morning. The one thing she's sure of is that she and Magda need to get back to the castle and soon.

Loath as she is to break up the tryst taking place on the other side of the table, she knows she's going to have to. She's wondering how she's supposed to do this when Dracul stands abruptly. "Luca, we must leave. Now!" His tone is demanding enough that it cuts through the haze surrounding Magda and his friend, with both of them blinking as though unsure of where they are.

Dracul walks around to the other side of the table, and tugs his friend to his feet. However, before he can drag him from the tavern, the guy pulls Magda into a tight embrace and kisses her as though their lives depend on it. He then jerks back as though burned and allows his friend to lead him from the tavern.

Magda is a mess and if Frankie didn't know better, she'd think her friend was intoxicated. However, the nearly full tankard in front of the vamp says otherwise. As gently as she can, Frankie leads Magda outside and transports them back to the castle.

They arrive back in Frankie's room to find Dex is still asleep. A good thing too, with Frankie needing to get rid of their disguises. Only then does she magic herself and Magda to the woman's room high up in one of the towers. Having tucked her friend up in bed, Frankie returns to her room for a few hours' sleep.

What a night. And what a shame Magda isn't able to make her own choice when it comes to a life mate. She deserves someone like the guy she met in the tavern tonight and not some crusty old man. It's wrong on so many levels.

It takes longer than it should for Frankie to fall asleep. Her mind is churning with images of Magda walking down the aisle in the crypt. She's on the arm of a guy who could pass for a cadaver on a good day.

7

Frankie is sure she's only just closed her eyes when Dex rouses her in the morning. She's a little the worse for wear. Not because she'd over-indulged on the local brew, but simply from a lack of sleep. Three hours tops by her calculations.

Sick of waiting for her to wake up properly, Dex pulls out the big guns. "I hear they have bacon downstairs."

It's not enough to cut through the sleep still clinging to Frankie.

"And coffee," he sing-songs.

The temptation of caffeine has her standing and blinking her eyes to clear them of sleep soon after. That she's swaying gently attests to how sleepy she still is. "Coffee? Did you say coffee?"

On walking into the hall, it becomes obvious all the others have been waiting for her. Perhaps the most surprising thing is how alert and awake Magda looks. They'd gone to bed around the same time, but perhaps Magda's dreams were more pleasant than Frankie's own?

The last thing Frankie does before they all walk downstairs is to check on Anne. There's no change, with the woman still flat on her back snoring loudly. Magda really did a number on her when she sucked all the energy out of the cottage.

It serves her nefarious, piratical relative right. The woman shouldn't have hitchhiked on the back of Frankie's spell like she did. Even though Magda could have her conscious again without blinking, Frankie refuses to give permission for this to happen. While celebrating the Winter Solstice at Castle Rhaetian isn't exactly as she'd hoped for, it's a heck of a lot better with Anne Bonny out cold.

Even so, Frankie's unsure what will greet them downstairs. Half-conscious energy vamps draped over every flat surface? Perhaps vamps staggering around suffering from energy hangovers? What?

She's also a little on edge about running into the guy who wants to eat her heart. Despite what Magda might say and the dude's husky voice, the words speak for themselves. Don't they? Frankie happens to be fond of her heart and would rather keep it intact for the holidays. Actually stitch this; she'd like it intact for ever.

She's therefore surprised on following Magda down a narrow hall to the right of the solstice tree to enter a room that's bright and sunny. It's also a complete contrast to everywhere else they've been allowed.

That there are two people sitting at a large table that could easily seat one-hundred diners is a further relief. Even better, neither of them is male and neither of them is Natalia. That woman would be guaranteed to give you indigestion.

Frankie is thinking the morning can't get any better when she spots a large sideboard groaning with covered dishes. She follows Magda in their direction, and her nostrils are assailed by the aroma coming off the contents. It's enough to have her salivating and Dex spinning next to the sideboard in anticipation.

Sure enough on lifting the first lid Frankie is faced with a mountain of fluffy scrambled eggs, the next holds bacon, followed by hash browns, sausages and even grilled tomatoes. As with hotel breakfast bars the world over, there are also bowls of cereal and fresh fruit on offer that look to be untouched. The one thing conspicuous by its absence is coffee with there being no espresso machine or filter coffee in sight. Jinxed jellyfish, she'd been looking forward to a cup of coffee.

Not being human or vamp, Zane and Dex aren't allowed to sit at the main table with it contravening some cultural law. However, they're soon set up at what looks to be the kids' table, with a cooked breakfast apiece. That Zane is chowing down on bacon appears to strike the two women sitting at the other end of the large expanse of oak as hilarious. Frankie has to agree it is tending to cannibalistic.

The one person not eating is Magda. Instead she's made herself a pot of coffee using hot water from a samovar that's industrial in size. Frankie didn't even know you could make real coffee using this method. While the samovar might be big, the coffee cup and saucer Magda's also collected are ridiculously small.

On seeing Magda pour her first cup, Frankie understands the reason for the china being as small as it is. The brew is dark and sludgy enough that even one cup would have Frankie bouncing off the rafters for the remainder of the day. If Magda intends to down the whole pot, she'll be capable of flight. Stifling another yawn, Frankie rethinks drinking coffee you can cut with a knife and jumps up to get herself a cup.

Frankie, Colin and Magda sit close to the table Dex and Zane are at so as include them in the conversation. Better this than having to repeat everything later and risk missing something out.

Her dad is the first to finish his breakfast, sitting back and rubbing his stomach contentedly. "What's the plan for tonight, Magda?" Rather than give her time to reply he continues. "When I was a boy my mom and my three great aunts used to bid the Crone farewell and invite the Maiden back into our lives."

"Yes! We 'ave similar ritual. Natalia, she undertake all the roles."

Yeah, of course she does, vainglorious creature. Frankie can't help but roll her eyes, although she's careful to hide this from Magda.

Careful, Shortcake.

Frankie straightens in her seat. She can't work out if Zane has seen her roll her eyes or heard her thought. Either way, he's right to warn her to be careful. Who knows what powers the old biddy that runs the place has? A quick glance at Magda, her dad and the two diners at the other end of the table shows no reaction to Zane's words that Frankie can see. Didn't they hear him?

Did you deliberately keep your words private then? Rather than speak the words telepathically to Zane as she would when she's communicating with Dex, Frankie imagines herself sending them to him. It's odd that she and Zane should be able to communicate like this now. She doesn't remember this being the case with the real Spud, and definitely not the real Zane.

Zane responds to her with thoughts of his own. *I was trying to. Testing, testing, one, two THREE!!!*.

The words come through loud and clear in Frankie's head, with Zane even shouting the last word to test their theory. Frankie casually looks around. Nope, if anyone else has heard him, they're not letting on. Even Dex, who's quick to respond to any telepathic message, hasn't stopped eating. Okay, so not the best test. He does like his food. A lot

Conscious she's been quiet for too long, Frankie joins in with Magda and her dad on their discussion of all things solstice. Frankie's only ever celebrated the summer solstice, so what happens at this time of the year is a mystery to her. "What's the story with the tree? Isn't that a Christmas tradition?"

"Pah! Not originally," says Colin. "The tree represents protection, prosperity and renewal. We opt for the fir because it's an evergreen, staying strong throughout the winter."

"It is as Colin says. Even the little creatures of our land celebrate the tree."

Frankie turns to Magda. "Little creatures?"

"The faeries. We always invite them to 'elp us celebrate."

Frankie's on her feet before she's conscious of standing, grabbing the back of her chair for support. "Show me, show me!" Not since she was a little kid and got given a *Malibu Barbie* for her birthday has Frankie been this excited about something so seemingly trivial.

Magda looks perplexed and amused in turn. "But Frankie, you must 'ave seen them. They are all over the tree."

"But... but I thought they were lights. Are you freaking kidding me?" She's halfway across the room, when Magda screams, stopping Frankie in her tracks.

"Not on your own!"

Frankie turns and looks at Magda. Only on seeing her expression of horror does she realize how serious her friend is about this. That the two women at the other end of the table are also on their feet and halfway over to her, tells of them running to her rescue too. However, on resuming her seat, Frankie's unnerved to see they look disappointed she's staying where she is rather than relieved.

It seems to take an age before everyone has finished their breakfast, including seconds in the case of Dex. Finally they're able to leave the room as a group and go check out the solstice tree in more detail. It's whilst walking back through into the entrance hall that Frankie spots a bunch of mistletoe hanging above the door.

She points up at it. "Wow, mistletoe. Is that a solstice thing too?" What a shame Zane isn't in his usual human form. At thoughts of kissing a pig, a giggle erupts unbidden; resulting in all of them looking at her like she's slipped a cog.

Don't worry, Shortcake. I'll make up for it when we get back to Seattle.

This thought from Zane has Frankie thanking her lucky stars the narrow hallway is gloomy. Better this than reveal her face and hair color now match. She's got to be way more careful with her errant thoughts if she wants to keep anything secret from Zane. Even thinking this has her mind going into overdrive with all the thoughts she'd like to keep from him.

Frankie looks down at him, unsure if he's

heard any of her thoughts. He's giving nothing away and is poker faced — or should that be porker faced — in the extreme.

Rather than letting Colin get the lead on the ins and outs of mistletoe, Magda rushes in. She tells of the small plant being associated with peacemaking and the end of discord. It's the connection to prosperity and fertility that's led to the tradition of kissing under it. Her dad nodding in agreement says this too is his take on mistletoe.

Frankie peers at the sprig of greenery held together with a bright red ribbon. *Should collect it all and make a party hat for the old girl?* Yet again, the only member of the group who hears this thought is Zane.

Might not be a bad idea. She looks like she could use some cheering up.

"My family collects it under waxing moon and we feed to our animals to guarantee fertility. We used to sacrifice the pair of white bulls, but white bulls they are very rare."

Frankie has to button her lips to stop from asking why the sacrifices have stopped. Is it because Natalia can't round up enough color-coordinated livestock, or that she wants to prevent their extinction? Frankie's leaning toward the former.

Dex looks up at Magda, his mouth hanging open. *"What, no barbeque?"*

The vamp turns to Frankie, knowing Dex has said something. "He is upset?"

"He's whining there won't be a barbeque with the bull tradition on hold."

Magda bends down and pats his head. "Relax Mr Dex, of course there will be feasting."

Back out in the entrance hall, Frankie urges the group toward the large tree, focusing on the nearest light as she walks closer. Sure enough, what looks like a sparking fairy light from a few feet back, shows itself to be a slumbering faerie on closer inspection. As tempting as it is to touch the small winged creature to see if it's real, Frankie holds back. She knows how annoyed she'd be is someone prodded her while she was having a nap and so she retreats slowly.

"That is so amazing. I had no idea they truly existed." Frankie deliberately keeps away from saying 'there's no such thing as faeries' to avoid the tree being blacked out and her responsible for faerie carnage. There must be thousands of the little creatures napping all over the tree.

"Come, we will leave them to their sleep so they are bright for tonight's celebrations." Magda turns and strides toward the back of the entrance hall, leaving the others to catch up.

When they do, Frankie is perplexed to find Magda facing what looks to be a solid wall. However, when the vamp pushes on the panel in front of her, it swivels to reveal a passageway. That half a dozen bats immediately swoop into the hall over their heads has Frankie and her dad ducking to avoid a tangle.

Dex weaves between their legs and scoots forward until he's half in and half out of the passageway. *"Cool, a secret passage."*

He's sniffing the floor and inching forward when Frankie puts a hand on his rump to stop his progress. "Hang on, mister. Hostess goes first." While this might sound like an issue of social niceties, Frankie's more worried her familiar will stumble into something he can't handle on his own. There are parts of this castle that are seriously weird. Okay, make that most parts of this castle.

Ignoring her request that the hostess go first, Zane totters through the sea of legs to join Dex. *"Where does it lead to?"*

"Come. I show you." Magda inches past Dex and Zane and proceeds to flip on an old-fashioned light switch. For a second nothing happens. Then the bulbs build in strength until it's possible to see along the passageway. At least until it slowly curves off to the left. That there's a downward slant is a bit of a worry.

"Are we going to the dungeons?" Dex backs up, jamming himself between Frankie's legs. *"I don't want to go to the dungeons."*

"I doubt it, Dex. Let me check." Frankie really needs to look through her late mom's spell book for that incantation. While Dex can run off at the mouth, giving out information she'd rather was kept private, it's a pain being stuck as his translator. The spell in question would allow everyone magical to hear his thoughts. This being both a good and bad thing, she's torn. "Dex wants to know if we're going to the dungeons. He's not keen."

Magda's laughter fills the narrow space, and it takes a minute for her to get her giggles under control enough to speak. "No, we go to stables. You like sleigh ride, yes?"

There follows a chorus of yes, both verbal and telepathic that confirms everyone is up for this.

8

This isn't quite what Frankie expected when Magda suggested a sleigh ride. Yep, they're in a sleigh and it's being pulled by a pair of matching jet-black stallions through a winter wonderland. What she hasn't expected is Magda sucking the energy from any wolf she sees as a late breakfast of sorts. No wonder she stuck with coffee earlier.

"Will they be okay?" Even though Frankie isn't a fan of large hairy animals with big teeth, she doesn't like the idea of them dying out here.

Magda stops her breakfast and looks at Frankie aghast. "I no kill them. I take enough to stop them attacking us. They wake verrry soon."

Dex, who's bouncing up and down on the

rump of the stallion on the right, whips his head around. That he nearly falls off his precarious perch has Frankie holding him in place with a quickly cobbled together spell. *"They can attack us?"*

"They can attack us?" repeats Frankie for Magda's benefit.

Rather than match his unease, Magda shrugs. "Of course. They are wild animals."

The joy sucked out of his adventure, Dex is soon on the floor of the sleigh. Not content with this, he noses beneath the furs Frankie's huddled under to save herself from frostbite. That Zane is already under there means it's a bit of a tight squeeze.

"Breakfast at three o'clock," says Colin, casually, taking Frankie's attention away from her ankles and back to their surroundings.

Magda smiles, displaying her pointy teeth. "Thank you, Mr Colin." There follows some more crackling and the wolf that's snapping worryingly close to her dad's elbow, passes out, landing in a tumbled heap in the snow.

This carries on until every wolf they see is lifeless.

"Ah, *Baba* has already been 'ere. We go now."

Baba? That's right the evil harridan, Natalia.

After this, the sleigh ride is less eventful from a being attacked by wild animals' standpoint. This isn't to say it isn't unsettling, with more and more unconscious wolves littering the sides of the trail. The closer they get to the castle, the worse it becomes. With the stone walls in sight, Frankie's horrified to see wolves lying in groups of three and four.

Unable to leave them as they are, Frankie throws small warming spells at them as they whiz by, in hopes of saving them from freezing to death. Frankie's gut is telling her the small, dark woman wouldn't give a rat's if the wolves died courtesy of her having a big breakfast.

The rest of the day is spent touring the castle itself and generally taking it easy. The way Magda tells it, the celebrations tonight will go on until the small hours of the following morning. If they're to last the distance, they need to catch up on their sleep. Especially Frankie.

Despite being on high alert, Frankie hasn't spotted the three men who'd been at the cottage the day before. The same three who'd hugged Magda at the bottom of the stairs. One of them is her stalker, but with all of them looking capable of ripping her heart out of her chest and chowing down on it, which one?

While Magda and Natalia might subsist on pure energy; this isn't to say all the vamps feed this way. Even though Frankie is trying not to be negative about the whole heart eating line, it smacks of O positive.

Thanks to an incredibly late night and all this running around, Frankie's ready for a nap come late afternoon and the others are drooping too. The one member of the group still bubbling with energy is Magda, with various farmyard and wild animals snoozing as a result. After escorting them to the top of the stairs, Magda flies back down them, throwing a, "Don't go anywhere without me," over her shoulder as she goes.

"I'll catch you later, *Pumpkin*." Frankie watches her dad disappear into the room he's sharing with Zane.

Dex, who's already wandered into the TV room, calls out to Frankie telepathically. *"Mom, can I watch that Lassie movie we saw bits of last night?"*

"Sure you can, buddy. I'll get it started for you."

Back from having settled Dex down with his 'puppy porn', Frankie finds Zane still waiting in the hallway. *Do you have a moment?*

Frankie nods and leans against the wall.

Not out here.

Frankie arches away from the wainscoting and walks into her room with Zane right behind her. That he scoots around her ankles and pushes the door to with his snout, alerts her to this being a conversation best not overheard. Even though their thought transfer appears to be covert, it would seem he doesn't want to take any chances.

I have a confession to make.

Okay. Frankie plonks herself down on the floor next to him with the plush rug making this more comfortable than she's expected.

Zane sits next to her. *I didn't just come along to protect you.*

Frankie has to smile although she's careful not to grin to widely. The idea that a runt pig would be any form of defense is laughable. Being the one responsible for his current disguise she doesn't want to annoy him too much by giving into giggles.

I still have my magic. That's as strong as ever.

You do? But I haven't seen you perform any. Even though she's just stated this as being a fact, Frankie thinks back on their time since she disguised him as a small piggy familiar. Nope, she's coming up empty.

Trust me, it's there. Zane demonstrates by pointing a trotter at the large blanket box at the end of the bed. That he's able to levitate it all around the room, before putting it safely back down, shows the truth of it.

What is it you wanted to tell me about?

Zane starts the thought transfer with his revelations making Frankie glad she's on the floor. Having heard his story, she'd be there, anyway. No wonder he's so transfixed with the silver mermaid on the top of the fir tree in the hall, it belongs to his people.

Not that it's a mere trinket. Without the Cleodora relic we can't bury those who have passed.

Frankie's unable to stop images of dead mermaids and mermen tethered to clumps of seaweed from cluttering her mind. Zane's expression tells her he's seeing these too. Bejinxed bunnies, she has got to remember to keep a handle on her thoughts.

This includes my parents.

Frankie's smile droops as she imagines how horrified she'd have been if she wasn't able to bury her mom earlier that same year.

But how are you going to get hold of it?

Sure Zane's got wings courtesy of her disguise, but piggy trotters will be useless for grabbing hold of something. Even more so when that something is a heavy hunk of silver. While it might look insignificant from ground level, Frankie knows this is in comparison to the freaking huge tree. Up close she imagines the relic will be close in size to a Skipjack Tuna.

Turns out rather than holding onto it, Zane's going to levitate the statue as he's just done with the blanket box. At the height of the festivities, he'll grab it, hide it and then rejoin the party as though nothing has happened. Simple enough, right?

Hang on a second. If you can access your full powers why don't you simply zap the relic from the top of the tree a second before we leave?

Zane squirms before he replies, alerting Frankie to this being a doozy. *Because the Cleodora is immune to that kind of magic. Only by being close and using a simple spell will I be able to move it. It has always been this way to stop it being stolen.*

Frankie doesn't need to say anything with the expression on Zane's face saying it all. Perhaps the Nautilus should invest in better security when Zane gets the relic back home?

Won't that mean there's a chance the Zilonkas can discover the real one is missing while we're still here? Turns out Zane has already thought of this with his plan being to create a replica of the mermaid. Frankie doesn't even try to hide her thoughts as to how ticked off Natalia will be at Zane taking the relic back. Never mind her family had stolen the relic two hundred and fifty years earlier. From their standpoint they'd see it as theirs now.

It takes as long as the Lassie movie for Zane and Frankie to finalize their plan, including how to keep the faerie lights quiet about what's going on. That this is up to Frankie doesn't sit well with her. *But what if I accidentally hurt them? Everyone knows if one fairy light goes out they all die. What if faerie lights are the same? I don't like those odds.*

You need to trust your powers. You're stronger than you think.

Frankie knows he's right. However, after years of having her powers fail when she needed them most, tentative doesn't begin to describe her un-willingness to use them on such a delicate matter. Heck, she just learned faeries are for real; she doesn't want to be the one responsible for their demise within twenty-four hours of doing so.

There's one more thing we need to take care of, Shortcake.

"What's that?"

I don't know about you, but I'd rather know what everyone is talking about. I'm good with languages, and yet I don't have a clue what half the people in this place are saying.

Zane has a point, it's been something that's been bothering Frankie too. And she only speaks English. "What can we do about it?"

Ever hear of a babel spell?

Despite her reservations about taking back the mermaid, Frankie agrees knowing Zane needs the relic to be able to bury his parents. It's this that sees Frankie with her wand hidden up the sleeve of her gown when they head downstairs later. Her relief at seeing the tube sleeves on the gorgeous forest green dress Magda had delivered to her room earlier in the evening had been heartfelt. Frankie hadn't thought to pack formal, simply stuffing warm clothes into her bag before their hurried departure.

Colin meantime is wearing a tuxedo that smacks of Dracula and for good reason with it on loan from a member of Magda's family. Even Dex and Zane are sporting small forest green bow ties that are cute enough that Frankie insists on a group photo at the bottom of the stairs.

Once again the entrance hall is empty but for

their small party. The difference this time is that it isn't deadly quiet. A rumble of voices fills the space, a lot of them, interspersed with bursts of laughter. Hmmm, Natalia must be telling jokes if the forced nature of the laughter is any indicator.

Frankie's already walking in the direction of the hallway next to the fir tree when Magda calls to her. "We are in the Great 'all tonight."

Great Hall? Frankie thinks the breakfast room is pretty grand, so who knows how stupendous the Great Hall must be. She walks gracefully back to join the others, struggling a little with the yards of fabric that make up the skirts of her formal gown.

For a jeans and boots kinda girl, the dress is a challenge. Here's hoping they don't need to make a run for it when Zane swipes the mermaid from the top of the tree. This is the last rational thought Frankie has for the next five minutes. 'Great' doesn't do the room justice. It's like the hall at Hogwarts, but twice the size.

Can she imagine white bulls being sacrificed in a setting like this? Heck yes she can. Heads of your enemies on pikes? Yep, they'd fit right in. Natalia stands on a dais at the other end of the huge space, decked out in dark red, presumably so the blood doesn't show. Gone is the crown of plaited hair, replaced with a sparkling gold one that's studded with jewels. Frankie doubts they're of the costume variety.

"Welcome to our hall!" Natalia's voice booms loudly for such a small woman.

It has the desired effect in that everyone turns to look at Frankie and the others. Not one to hog the limelight this has Frankie dying a little inside. Exactly as Natalia no doubt intended.

Stand tall. Do not cower before this... this woman.

So loud and authoritative are Zane's words in Frankie's head that her back is ramrod straight soon after. She stops looking at the floor and instead directs her gaze at Natalia. Well not directly. Who knows if those rumors about vampires being able to hypnotize you are true?

Instead she looks at the woman's crown. From this distance the personification of evil won't be able to tell the difference. That she'll still take Frankie's supposed eye contact as a direct challenge is confirmed by Magda sucking her breath in so hard it results in a coughing fit.

Frankie uses this as an excuse to turn to the side, patting Magda on the back enough to help her start breathing properly again.

"Thank you. Come, we sit now."

Frankie doesn't bother looking to the front of the hall again. Instead she follows Magda and the others to seats at the end of one of the three large tables. Perhaps large is an understatement. Each table is long enough to seat two hundred diners. Once Frankie and the others are seated, all three tables are full to capacity.

That Frankie and the others are closest to the door says more than anything what their social standing is at this gathering. She's quite happy with their place in the pecking order as it'll make it far easier to sneak out when the time comes.

Only when they're all seated, with Zane and Dex at a small table close by, does Frankie relax somewhat. This is until she turns to say good evening to the man sitting next to her. Bejinkers he's cute! It's only after she's had this thought that she thinks she should have kept it to herself. *Sorry, but he is.* Frankie shuts her thoughts up in an effort at damage control, then decides her silence isn't enough. *Not as cute as you, of course.*

Of course. There's no missing the sarcasm in Zane's response.

Even sitting down, Frankie can tell the man next to her is tall. Certainly he's a lot taller than her or Zane.

Okay, I get it. He's cute AND he's tall.

Frankie closes her eyes trying to get control of her thoughts, thinking of them as being barricaded inside her head rather than free to roam. *Internal memo, keep your thoughts to yourself.* Not getting a response from Zane, Frankie knows she's been successful.

Aware her dinner companion is watching her while she wrangles with this internal conflict, Frankie turns back to him. "I'm Frankie."

"This I know. I am Dominik."

Frankie would know the voice anywhere; she'd even heard it in a dream last night. Without a slab of wood between them the effect on her nerves is even more spectacular. Sure she'd mused that a makeover would work wonders on the three wild men who'd crashed through the cottage door; never could she have envisaged a change so dramatic.

He's clean-shaven and his shoulder-length dirty blond hair has been cut so it just kisses the collar of his tux. It's a deadly combination.

His eating her heart is no longer as scary as it had been when he'd first voiced the suggestion. This isn't to say her heart is safe. His caressing her with dark brown eyes while licking his full lips has the organ in question stopping dead in her chest.

9

I t's only Zane coughing telepathically, and loudly, inside her head that brings Frankie back to her surroundings. She even manages to squeak out a credible, "Nice to meet you." She then locks her gaze on Magda who's sitting on the other side of the table, next to Frankie's dad.

"He is my cousin, 'e is best avoided."

Ha, it's all very well for Magda to say that when Frankie's the one stuck next to the guy for however many hours.

"She is not serious. I am a kitten."

Frankie isn't sure if he's said this in English or his own peculiar dialect. Either way she understands him perfectly, and she's not buying his story. She skews her gaze in his direction, managing to avoid direct eye contact. "Kitten? Of course you are." Okay, so he had almost purred the last few words, but seriously a kitten? More like a blinkin' mountain lion or a jaguar, or some other feline with big teeth who likes to tease their prey.

Despite her concerns, Dominik is the perfect dinner companion, explaining the ceremony to Frankie as Natalia moves through it. All eyes on her, the woman positively glows, no doubt because she's stealing energy from everyone in the room. Frankie, however, can't feel herself being drained. Looks as if the double wards she and her dad put in place are working out just as they planned.

The problem with all the attention Frankie's receiving from Dominik is that it's making it difficult for her to find an opportunity to slip away. She needs to freeze the faeries so Zane can retrieve the silver mermaid without them kicking up a fuss. She sure as frozen faeries can't do that from in here. She puts her wine glass back down on the table and is surprised to see it's empty. Again. It does however give her an idea as to how she can escape the room briefly. And with Dex already asleep under the small table he's sharing with Zane, the timing couldn't be better.

"Excuse me. I need to, ah…" How on earth do you explain to a gorgeous vampire that you need to visit the bathroom? Frankie gives up, instead turning to Magda and pulling a face that spells out to her friend that she needs to leave the table for a comfort stop. Her jerking her head toward the door probably helps too.

Without a word, Magda gets to her feet and pushing her seat back, turns toward the doors. Frankie follows suit. The one thing that Frankie does that Magda doesn't do is swish the hem of her gown over the top of Zane as they pass by. He disappears without trace amid the acres of silky green fabric, and with some fancy footwork on his part, stays this way until they're out in the hall.

On seeing a small snout poking out from under the hem of her gown, Frankie twitches the fabric hard, giving Zane the message to stay put.

If Magda has seen anything, she hasn't reacted. "Come I show you the bathroom."

Frankie follows her friend across the hall toward the passage that leads to the breakfast room. That this has them close to the fir tree is perfect. Frankie whips her wand out of her sleeve, points it at the tree and repeats the spell she practiced in her room.

All the lights on the tree fizzle and pop leaving Frankie holding her breath. She releases it in a rush and hurries to catch up with Magda only after they're all glowing brightly again. Whether she's managed to freeze the small creatures, they're about to find out. The one thing she knows for sure is that Zane has managed to get out from under her skirts and safely behind the fir tree without being spotted.

Rather than walking all the way to the room they'd eaten breakfast in that morning, they stop halfway and Magda slides open yet another secret panel. Rather than gloom on the other side as had been the case with the passage that led to the stables, here everything is modern and white. It's different to the dark oak, non-flush bathroom fixtures and fittings Frankie's been expecting in this part of the castle.

I really didn't need that image, Shortcake.

"I will wait for you out in the entrance 'all."

"No!" Frankie hasn't meant to be as forceful in her plea, and it's something that shows on her friend's face. "It's just that I might need help with my dress." It's the first excuse Frankie can think of to keep Magda from returning to the hall and seeing Zane's bait and switch. Looking at the mountain of satin and the small cubicle has her realizing her friend staying is a necessity in more ways than one.

It takes both of them rearranging all that fabric

for Frankie to be able to answer the call of nature without her flushing her skirts in the process. Even safely out of the cubicle it takes Magda's help to ensure her skirts are where they should be. Thoughts of returning to the hall with the back of her dress tucked in somewhere aren't to be borne.

Her even thinking about this has Zane chuckling inside her head, stopping her thoughts in their tracks.

Finally, with everything as it should be, Magda and Frankie make their way back to the Great Hall. On passing the large fir, Zane sneaks back under Frankie's skirts in a well-practiced maneuver. On her walking past the small table set aside for him and Dex, Zane simply stops walking. The dress floats over him leaving him next to the table as if he's always been there. That the acres of material obscure this maneuver from those at the tables is simply a happy coincidence.

Frankie regains her seat next to Dominik all while keeping her expression as neutral as possible. Not that this has Magda's cousin ignoring her.

"The small winged pig. I take it he needed a break too?" That Dominik is keeping his voice low isn't lost on Frankie.

"Ah yes, he did." She replies at a similar volume. Let the hunky vamp make of it what he wants. What she's not sure of is whether the replica mermaid atop the tree will pass muster, or if the swap has even taken place. Here's hoping the running shoes Frankie's wearing under her gown don't prove necessary.

The evening is interminable, to the point Frankie needs to use the facilities two more times, again necessitating Magda's help. Not that the vamp needs Frankie to return the favor. The vamp's own dress is a sheath of black velvet, with a mid-thigh slit that makes everything a breeze.

It's five in the morning before the festivities wind down and Frankie's pleased to note Natalia's slurring her words. Of all the vamps in the hall, she's the one Frankie is most worried will notice a swap has taken place with the mermaid. As to where the real tree topper is, Frankie hasn't dared ask Zane. Even with their communications seemingly private, it's better she doesn't know. In case she ends up being tortured in the dungeons, for hours on end.

Stop it, Shortcake. Only freak out if you need to.

Dominik once again leans in close and whispers in her ear. "He is right. You need to stay calm."

Frankie stiffens in her seat and she sees even Zane looks to be frozen in place. She thinks briefly about trying to brazen her way out of it. The merest peek in Dominik's direction and she knows he's heard Zane as clearly as she has herself. Whether he has any idea what they've been discussing is another story.

Before she allows herself to think about it, she imagines a virtual tinfoil hat protecting her thoughts and keeping them inside her head. Only when this is in place does she give her imagination and memories full rein. Their main discussion about the mermaid had been on the top floor. Surely if Dominik had heard them planning the heist he'd have said something by now, even if just to Frankie or Magda?

What are they supposed to do? Frankie hasn't come up with a solution when she hears movement at the other end of the hall. On looking up she can see the Queen Bee — make that Queen Vee — is ready to retire for the night, make that day. What if she walks past Dominik? Surely he'll say something.

Dominik's breath on her neck is hot, his words warm. "Your secret is safe with me, Ta ha zemrën."

Frankie waits for the 'but'.

"But, I shall expect payment for my silence."

And there it is.

Without sending thoughts her way, she can tell just by looking at Zane that he's rigid in an effort to stop himself from using magic against Magda's cousin. He needs to hold on for another half hour or so. Frankie stares at Dominik, holding his gaze until Natalia has safely walked the length of the hall and out through the double doors next to Zane and Dex.

The Zilonka matriarch out in the hallway, it's make-or-break time. Or perhaps even run like heck time. Will she look up and notice the switch? Will she somehow sense it? Will Dominik take his payment and then break his silence, anyway? Magda said he wasn't to be trusted.

All of this is soon rendered moot.

"Thief! Stop! Thief!" There's no doubt the person screaming is Natalia, simply because of the sheer volume. Who she's screaming at, Frankie can't imagine. Even the quickest of checks has shown Zane to be standing on the small table set aside for him and Dex.

The shouting is enough to wake the small dog who's been fast asleep under the table working on digesting a meal big enough for a grown man. *"What's happening? What'd I miss?"* Still half asleep, Dex comes close to be trampled by a couple of guards running in answer to Natalia's continued yelling. It's enough to have him scoot back under the safety of the table.

Not wanting to miss out on the action, Frankie is soon on her feet. She hitches her dress up at the front to avoid it catching on anything and marches out into the hall. The scene that greets her has her dropping the hem and hiding her inappropriate footwear. She's soon joined by the others, with the five of them hugging a wall to avoid the worst of the mayhem.

Frankie looks at the top of the fir tree. "But she was asleep. I checked in on her before we came down for dinner." The one plus so far as Frankie can see is that Anne looks as hideous as she'd hoped in the rhubarb pink thermal underwear.

"Jack! I need help!" Anne's words as she clutches the silver mermaid to her chest while swaying backward and forward atop the tree are as loud as Natalia's. Frankie isn't sure how Calico Jack — her grandpa and Anne's de facto partner — is supposed to help. Frankie and the others couldn't have reached the castle without Magda's help. How is Jack supposed to get himself there?

Natalia is having none of it. "No one steal from me. Bring me axe. I cut tree down myself."

Frankie didn't see this coming. Surely the tree

is sacrosanct? Won't it bring bad luck, not to mention a few breakages, if the crazy vamp chops the blasted thing down inside the castle?

She's no closer to a conclusion when one of the castle guards hands Natalia an axe. Its size should make it impossible for the diminutive woman to pick it up, let alone swing the monster. But no, she's up to the challenge and the sound of her first strike at the base of the tree echoes around the hall. This is followed by another, and another.

Despite Frankie having walked past the fir tree several times on her trips to and from the bathroom, she hasn't yet been able to unfreeze the faeries. Magda has stayed too close to allow her to get her wand, never mind use it. It's this that sees faeries raining down, knocked off their perches by each successive swing of the axe.

It's something Frankie needs to rectify, not wanting them to be hurt on account of her. Standing side on to the tree, she slides her hand up her sleeve and touches the end of her wand. Frankie mutters the reversal spell, points her elbow and thus the wand at the tree and is relieved to see the faeries flicker into life. They then lift as a group and flee the hall with the precision of an aerobatics squad.

None of this slows Natalia; she's on a mission,

with Anne and the silver mermaid in her sights. At first Frankie thinks she's imagining things, even blinking to make sure her eyes aren't deceiving her. They're not. Anne screaming Jack's name over and over, has resulted in a shimmering circle of light floating above the heads of the crowd. It's one that's growing more obvious all the time.

Guests start moving back to avoid standing under this anomaly showing Frankie she's not alone in seeing it. Some even flee the hall altogether. Anne however looks to be delighted by its appearance. Ignoring the demented woman hacking away at the base of the tree, Anne stands tall on one of the upper branches. It looks as if all those years living on sailing ships are coming in handy with her balance rock-solid. Frankie's grandmamma then clasps the Cleodora relic tight against her chest and without hesitation swan dives into the shimmering circle of light.

10

There's a stunned silence as the crowd watches the tall fir topple into the middle of the entrance hall. So horrified are they that most miss the fact Anne has made it through the shimmering circle of light. That she hasn't landed with a splat on the oak floor in front of them. Natalia is not among them.

Her quarry has escaped and the vamp queen is steaming mad. Something she demonstrates by burying the axe in the nearest wall and screaming like a banshee at a karaoke competition. Courtesy of the babel spell Frankie's able to understand every word of the rant that follows.

Something that needs no translation is the

woman dragging energy out of all those around her in order to feed her anger. What starts out as a slow Mexican wave of people falling unconscious to the floor soon speeds up.

Thanks to the double wards Frankie and her dad placed on everyone in their group, they're still standing long after others have succumbed. Of some surprise is that Magda's still on her feet alongside them. Is this all down to her being in the cottage when they enacted the spell? They'd thrown enough of their powers at it that it could well have protected people in the vicinity and not just those in Frankie's room.

Frankie only realizes Zane the runt pig is no longer next to her when she sees him peeping through the bannister halfway up the stairs. Dex is next to him. *"Move it, Mom. Spud says it's time to leave."*

Frankie's frozen where she is, unable to move, waiting for Natalia to turn in her direction. Who knows if the spell will hold if she's the sole target of the evil woman? Fortunately she doesn't get to find out. Dominik, also unaffected by Natalia's energy-sapping tantrum, pops up next to her. He grabs her hand and drags her in the direction of the stairs. She's pleased on looking back to see Magda and her dad are following in their wake.

The trance broken, Frankie yanks her hand free of Dominik's. She then takes hold of the front of her dress, lifting it high and taking the stairs two at a time. Magda and Colin likewise are sprinting up the stairs behind her. Their sole aim is to reach the top floor and get away from the castle before leaving isn't an option.

On arriving in the attic space, Dominik pulls a battered piece of mistletoe from the pocket of his tux and holds it above Frankie's head. He then claims a chaste kiss, something that surprises her. *Perhaps he's a kitten after all?* The sultry smile he bestows upon her, says otherwise. "My fiery one, time is not on our side. You must go. I will see you soon to collect on my promise."

He's lucky he then races back down the stairs because a certain little piggy has a trotter pointed to where he'd just been standing. Taking in the squint in Zane's eyes Frankie doubts he would have held back, either. Frankie's dad having grabbed his bag marches into her room. All of them in there, Frankie slides the three bolts home and readies herself to repeat the words Magda gives her.

· · ·

Reaching the safety of Pier 51 back in Seattle is almost a let-down after their adrenalin fueled escape from Castle Rhaetian. Frankie drops her bag on the dock, puts Dex down next to it and pulls Magda into a tight embrace. "Thank you for everything you did back there. Can you say thanks to Dominik too?"

Frankie would love it if her friend was staying in Seattle, but knows this can't happen. The aura of sadness that surrounds Magda confirms the vamp is returning to the castle to face up to her commitments. What awaits her there has a shiver running up and down Frankie's spine. To heck with it, she has to say something. Anything.

"You don't need to do this. I could disguise you so your family would never find you."

"I... I cannot do this. To do so would shame my family."

"But what about..." Frankie runs out of words, not remembering the name of the man Magda had met at the tavern.

"My beautiful Luca. My memories, they will keep me warm through the cold nights."

That her friend's voice breaks on a sob has Frankie fighting to get her own tears under control. She squeezes her friend extra tight. "Send me a sign if you change your mind. Promise?"

Frankie gets a jerky nod in response with Magda's words looking to be jammed in her throat, as Frankie's own are now.

"Any chance you can sort me out?" Zane speaking to her telepathically rather than by thought transfer tells her he doesn't think anyone from the castle has followed them home.

"Yeah, sure. Hang on a sec." Frankie drags her wand out the sleeve of her borrowed gown and points it at the small pig. It's on seeing him back in his merman form that she's reminded how gorgeous he truly is. And he's definitely tall enough for her.

Careful Shortcake, not while we've got company.

Frankie gasps; unable to believe their ability to communicate by thought alone has stayed even though he's no longer masquerading as Spud. She's not sure if this is a good thing, or a bad one.

"Wait! What? Spud?" Confusion is writ large on Dex's face. *"But..."*

"Sorry Dex, we needed to keep it a secret. I hope you're okay with that?" To soften the blow of being kept out of the loop, Zane gives Dex a good, rough scratch up and down his back.

Only once Dex is placated, does Zane stand tall and give Magda a long hug. "Thank you for your hospitality, and your friendship. Sorry it ended as it did. You'll always have somewhere to stay at the Marina Coven, if you need to escape."

Frankie backs up his words with an offer of a place to stay. She's got plenty of room on her schooner and part of her thinks Magda is going to need somewhere to get away to.

Following a brief hug from Colin, who she doesn't know as well, Magda disappears to an accompaniment of tinkling bells, leaving Frankie wiping her eyes.

There then follows an awkward silence in which Frankie looks at Zane, unsure what's supposed to happen now. The silence extends for long enough that Colin coughs if just to break it. "Ah yes, well, I'll just leave you two alone. I have friends in Portland I need to visit." Before Frankie can tell him, he doesn't need to leave on their behalf; he's clicked his fingers and disappeared in a shower of sparks, leaving his bag behind.

The final sparks haven't hit the dock when Zane leans over and unzips Frankie's bag. That he then pulls the Cleodora relic from her bag shocks her. The bag hadn't felt heavy enough to be holding this much silver. And she was right to think the mermaid would be a lot bigger close up. The thing is much larger than should have been able to fit in her bag and have the zipper still close.

"I told you my magic was strong when I was in that disguise of yours." Zane leans down and kisses Frankie with a passion that has her toes curling although any heat generated is frozen by his next words. "I'm sorry, Shortcake. I need to return this to my people."

Even with her eyes still closed, Frankie knows he's dived into the harbor. Apart from the sound of a large merman and a hunk of silver hitting the water, there's a humongous splash that drenches her up to her knees. What a rubbish ending to the holidays. Was her mom right to hate the Winter Solstice after all?

After throwing a drying spell at the bottom of her gown, Frankie bends over and picks up the two bags. Unable to click her fingers without putting them back down, she trudges to the end of the pier and onto the *Pearl*. On walking into her cabin, she's struck anew by how sadly lacking in seasonal cheer it is.

"What? Where's the yule altar gone?" Frankie distinctly remembers it still being there when they left for Castle Rhaetian.

As if to double check, Dex stretches until he's on tip toes and his nose is edging over the top of the sideboard. *"Maybe he took it with him to his friend's place."*

"Perhaps he did." Frankie yawns loudly. The adrenalin wearing off, exhaustion is setting in. Never mind the whole chopping down a solstice tree in your front hall debacle, last night had been a late one. It's this that soon sees her sprawled on her bed, still in the green dress, with Dex snuggled up beside her.

Neither of them is a box of birdies the following morning. While sleep had come easily due to exhaustion, Frankie's dreams were harder to deal with. These had left her thrashing around on her bed to the point Dex had decamped at some point during the night.

Struggling free of the dress, Frankie stands under the shower longer than she usually would; anything to rinse away the gloom that's made itself at home in her heart. She knows why she's feeling like this, not that this lifts her spirits. Dressed and with her hair dry enough to risk a quick trip outside, Frankie grabs her wallet.

"Do you want to stay here, or come to *Magic Beans* with me?" Even though coffee and baked goods won't have her any happier, she knows the caffeine and sugar might go some way to perking her up.

Dex yawns widely before hopping up onto her disheveled bed. He then turns around three times before collapsing. *"I'll wait here. I need to catch up on my sleep."*

"Blueberry?"

"Yes please, mom."

Stepping off the *Pearl* onto the dock, Frankie's surprised by how *lazy* the wind is, with it not bothering to go around, but rather straight through her. "Brazen barnacles it's freezing," says Frankie, to the empty dock. She then hurries its length making straight for *Magic Beans.*

On entering the café that's visible only to magical folk, Frankie's surprised to find Mac, the owner, is on his own. She would have expected a few more people to be back in their normal routine with the solstice celebrations all but over. "Hey Mac, how you doing?"

There's no need for Frankie to put in an order, with Mac already bagging up the muffins before getting on with her coffee. Often the proprietor knows better than she does herself, what it is she's hankering for.

"Good. And you?"

Rather than bring Mac's spirits down to her own level, Frankie's answer is deliberately vague. The roar of the espresso machine making conversation impossible, they fall silent. While Mac concentrates on finishing her coffee, Frankie thinks about what she's going to do to keep busy for the rest of the holidays.

Sure she could practice her spells, but this wouldn't be the same without Zane. He makes spell work fun. Not knowing where his 'people' live means she has no idea how long it's going to take him to get the Cleodora relic back and return to Seattle.

If he's got to bury his parents, he could be gone weeks. If there's as big a back log as he was making out, he could be gone months. It's these gloomy thoughts that have Frankie grabbing her coffee and the brown paper bag from Mac and transporting herself directly back to the *Pearl* rather than walking home. It's a much warmer option too.

Dex makes short work of his two muffins while Frankie polishes off her muffin and coffee in record time. She's hungry as a result of not eating much at dinner the night before. This had been down to nerves about the whole faerie freezing spell and not knowing what half the dishes were. Foreign and spicy, with lashings of offal seemed to be a common theme and to someone with pedestrian tastes like hers this isn't a great culinary pairing.

That she goes back to bed, not bothering to undress, reinforces how blue she's feeling. Her managing to fall asleep again tells how tired she still is.

She's got no idea how long she's been asleep when she's roused by someone knocking at her cabin door. All she knows is that it's dark outside. It must be her dad back from visiting his friends.

Frankie staggers to her feet and over to the door, swinging it wide to allow him to enter. Only it isn't her dad.

"You're back." Frankie wants to say more, but the words stick in her throat.

Why is she so uptight all of a sudden? Hasn't spending the solstice with Zane been what she wants? Now he's here, and she doesn't know what to say to him. What is wrong with her? It's thinking about this that has tears prickling her eyes and she's mortified when she chokes on a loud sob.

"Come here, you." Zane steps forward and drags her into a tight embrace, his chin resting on top of her head. "Did you think I wouldn't come back?"

Frankie gives up trying to put her thoughts into words, instead nodding in answer.

"Shortcake, I wouldn't leave you on your own. Not at this time of the year."

He goes to pull away, but Frankie holds on tight keeping him where he is. She's not ready for him to see her with puffy eyes and a runny nose this early in their relationship.

"How about you splash some cold water on your face? I've got something I want to show you."

Unable to stay clinging to him like a limpet until her face is back to normal; Frankie untangles herself and, staring studiously at the floor, flees to the safety of the bathroom and some much-needed repairs to her face.

On her return, she finds Zane stretched out on her bed, scratching Dex in all the places he can't reach on his own. Frankie already knew this was what was happening courtesy of Dex's running refrain of *"Don't stop, don't stop, oh please, please don't stop"*.

"Sorry, buddy. Your mom and I have something we need to do. We'll come get you soon." There's some grumbling from Dex, although this doesn't last long. They've not had time to leave the cabin before he rolls onto his back and falls asleep again.

Zane puts his finger to his lips before dragging Frankie into another embrace. However, there's no time to enjoy it, with him clicking his fingers and sending them over to his place. Frankie's glad they've arrived in the hallway of his houseboat as she hasn't had time to put a jacket on.

Zane pulls free of their embrace and, after a gentle kiss to her forehead, steers Frankie over to face the door that leads to the great room. "Okay, close your eyes."

Frankie complies, although the temptation to peek is irresistible.

"Are they closed? If they're not closed, I can't open the door."

Frankie nods and squeezes her eyes extra tight, just to be on the safe side.

She's aware of Zane leaning around her and opening the door and again she has to force herself to keep her eyes closed. He guides her forward half a dozen steps before stopping. Frankie's glad he's got his hands on her shoulders when this gives her the wobbles.

"Okay, you can open them."

Frankie's afraid to. What if it's a let-down?

"Come on, Shortcake, open them."

Frankie does and as worried as she's been that she'll be disappointed, she doesn't know what to think. Surely her eyes must be playing tricks on her? But no, her first impression was spot on. Every inch of the ceiling of the great room is covered in sprigs of mistletoe. This would be amazing on its own, with the hundreds of faeries nestled in amongst the greenery, sparkling and shining, it's magical.

Frankie walks around the room, dragging Zane with her. *How did he know?*

Because I know you, Frankie, that's how I knew.

Zane turns her gently around and points to the ceiling. He then cradles her face with his hands and his lips meet hers in a kiss that sears her soul. She's melting against him when he stops long enough to whisper in her ear.

Happy solstice, Frankie. Happy solstice.

It doesn't take much effort to ignore for the moment that she and Zane have to return to *Garnet Cove*. There are a lot of wrongly imprisoned magical folk in *All Hallows Keep* who are relying on them. Until then, they've got a lot of preparation (and mistletoe) to get through.

THANK YOU

For choosing my book from all those fantastic paranormal cozy mysteries out there! It's readers like you who allow me to pursue my career as a writer.

Lastly, don't be a stranger. I'm mostly online at Twitter, but I'm also on Facebook, Instagram (so many sunset and cat photos) and Pinterest. You'll find all the links on my website.

www.andrenelowauthor.com

ABOUT THE AUTHOR

Andie's love of writing was instilled in her by her mother, although if her mum was still alive, she'd be smacking Andie across the back of the head given the direction some of her writing has taken.

Irreverent, cutting and reflecting her background as a stand-up comic, it's edgy with humor that's a little off-the-wall in places.

Andie lives in the beautiful Hawke's Bay region of New Zealand, an area renowned for stunning scenery and great wine.

CPSIA information can be obtained
at www.ICGtesting.com
Printed in the USA
BVHW042245210720
584283BV00009B/88

9 780995 138988